"What do you want?"

"I don't know," he said slowly, as though she had surprised him.

Surprised herself, she lifted her face to discover him looking at her with something like astonishment, perhaps even a hint of resentment.

"I haven't been able to get you out of my mind. I'm not usually a gambler, but—occasionally I like to take a chance on something. You do, too, I think."

Was it time for her to allow this wild yearning for the forbidden?

"Yes," Kieran said, as though answering her unspoken question. "Shall we start again, Tegan?"

ROBYN DONALD lives in northern New Zealand with her husband and a Corgi dog. They love the outdoors and particularly enjoy sailing and stargazing on warm nights. Robyn doesn't remember being taught to read, but rates reading as one of her greatest pleasures, if not a vice. She finds writing intensely rewarding and is continually surprised by the way her characters develop independent lives of their own.

Books by Robyn Donald

HARLEQUIN PRESENTS
1464—SOME KIND OF MADNESS
1505—STORM OVER PARADISE
1537—THE GOLDEN MASK
1565—ONCE BITTEN, TWICE SHY
1577—THE STONE PRINCESS
1611—SUCH DARK MAGIC

HARLEQUIN ROMANCE
2391—BAY OF STARS
2437—ICEBERG

ROBYN DONALD

DONALD

Pagan Surrender

Harlequin Books

TORONTO • NEW YORK • LONDON
AMSTERDAM • PARIS • SYDNEY • HAMBURG
STOCKHOLM • ATHENS • TOKYO • MILAN
MADRID • WARSAW • BUDAPEST • AUCKLAND

ISBN 0-373-11639-X

PAGAN SURRENDER

CHAPTER ONE

THE vicious thunk of her slamming door dragged Tegan Jones's attention from the sketch she was making; doors normally whispered shut in this opulent decorator's office and showroom.

Pushing back a heavy wave of hair from one flushed cheek, she looked up, her straight dark brows drawing together. 'I gather it didn't go well.'

Alana Richmond flung her briefcase into a chair. 'No, it did not go well! Kieran Sinclair doesn't just *look* like a smouldering hero from some super-heated feminine fantasy about an arrogant, dangerous, masterful man, he *behaves* as though he believes the fantasy, too. He took one cursory look at this presentation that I've slaved over for *weeks*, and then he said——' she did her best to mimic a man's deep tones '—Ms Richmond, I can see *you* in these rooms perfectly, but not me.'

Tegan's face was very still, very composed. 'How very patronising,' she murmured, for lack of something better to say. A small trickle of moisture ran down her back. Although every window in the place was open, it was still hot inside, and far too humid. Blair teased Tegan because she refused to switch on the air-conditioning, and on this particular searing Friday morning she herself wondered whether perhaps she wasn't taking her principles a little too far.

No wonder everyone in Auckland who could wangle a holiday in January fled New Zealand's biggest city then, hieing off to the beach or the country or the mountains. Plenty remained, however; the roar of traffic down Newmarket's main street fifty metres away attested that the most newly fashionable of the city's suburbs was still busy in spite of the yearly exodus.

'Patronising? He was damned condescending.' Snorting, Alana dropped her small blonde self into another chair. 'Of course I knew it was too good to be true. I mean, such a gorgeous man—God, ten out of ten, I swear, body and face and all, and you know how rare that is! He's six feet four if he's an inch, with shoulders that go from one side of the room to the other, and he is *beautiful*.'

Tegan's grin hid the odd little tremor of her nerves that the thought of Kieran Sinclair caused. Yes, beautiful described him exactly. As perilously beautiful and as powerful as Lucifer, the fallen angel of darkness. 'All that and brains too,' she said, adding thoughtfully, 'At least, I suppose you need brains to be a merchant banker.'

'Brains or not, he's a condescending beast.' Alana looked down at her small, beringed hands. 'I feel as though I've let you both down,' she confided. 'This was to be my first big job here, and I've put the man off completely.'

Eight inches taller than the other woman's five feet two, and at twenty-eight five years younger, Tegan sometimes felt more like a senior prefect than a partner in the business that employed Alana. 'Don't worry about it; neither Blair nor I are going to hold it against you,' she said comfortingly. 'Every so often we get a difficult customer, and usually it's just a matter of

clashing personalities. Obviously we misread Kieran
Sinclair. You do the modern stuff perfectly, and he certainly seems the type to want that. What did he actually say about your presentation?'

'Not a lot, beyond the fact that it looked rather like
the inside of an ice-cream cake.'

Tegan's large topaz eyes lifted towards the ceiling.
She sighed, then grinned.

For the first time Alana smiled, although it was obvious that the summary dismissal of her decorating
scheme still rankled. 'I started to explain, and he just
cut me off. He said there wasn't a room he could see
himself living in, and that his house is seventy years old,
not some post-modern mansion knocked up in the last
two years. When I tried again he just gave me a condescending smile and said it was all very smart and very
chic, but he was neither smart nor chic, so it wouldn't
do for him. I started to say I'd nut out another scheme,
but he cut me off again. Then his secretary bustled me
out.' She brooded for a moment. 'Arrogant swine.'

Tegan made a sympathetic noise. 'You shouldn't have
given it to him cold—it never works. They always spend
ages picking holes in everything, totally ignoring the
fact that most of it is just what they asked for, and the
bits they find so objectionable can be changed.'

'I didn't have much choice. When the man says do
this, you do it! He has that steely air, a sort of crack of
command in his voice.'

Alana had put in a lot of work on Kieran Sinclair's
scheme, and it always hurt to be turned down, especially when it was as abrupt and mannerless as this had
been. But rejection happened often in the decorating
business. Tegan suspected that Alana was reacting so

strongly because she had rather fallen for Kieran Sinclair.

'Oh, well, I'd better go and tell Blair, I suppose,' Alana finished, heading for the door.

Tegan watched her leave the room, then looked down at her desk. Instead of colour swatches and cryptic notes, she saw Kieran Sinclair ten years before, his overwhelmingly handsome face stark with contempt as he looked down his straight nose at her.

And his voice, that deep, intriguing voice, shredding her miserable attempt at poise with freezing scorn. 'You cheating, lying little tramp,' he'd said in a barely audible voice. 'Why Sam had to fall for such a blatant opportunist I'll never know.'

'I'm sorry,' she'd whispered, so far out of her depth that she didn't know how to deal with it. 'I just don't love him enough to marry him.'

'Then why did you let him live in some fool's paradise?'

Tegan felt like a criminal. 'I didn't realise he was falling in love with me,' she muttered at last when it became obvious he wasn't going to let her off the hook.

It was the truth, but only part of it. She couldn't tell Sam's best friend it had never occurred to her that Sam, confined to a wheelchair for the rest of his life, unable to consummate a marriage, could fall in love. Young and thoughtless as she was, she hadn't intended to hurt Sam at all.

'Because he was rich.' Ice coated Kieran Sinclair's words, but it was the disdain in the blue-green eyes that stabbed Tegan through to the heart.

Wretchedly, impelled by a spark of determination to defend herself, she said, 'I'm sorry. I know I've behaved badly, but he assumed too much; I never said I was going to marry him, or even that was I was in love with him. I like him very much——'

'But you liked the money he lavished on you more!'

Her head drooped like a flower on a long stem. Although she had refused to accept presents from him Sam *had* lavished money on her, taking her to places she would never have been able to afford.

Kieran Sinclair said unforgivably, 'In my book that's prostitution, and of the worst sort, because you didn't even have to go to bed with him! Not that any normal man would find your couple of yards of body particularly attractive.'

At eighteen Tegan had been thin, still not confident in her height, and inclined to be awkward. Although she had filled out a lot since then, she could still feel the disparaging, derisory survey he'd subjected her to. She had wanted to die of humiliation. But worse was to follow. Kieran Sinclair's smile made her blood run cold. In a voice made all the more memorable because of its quiet, implacable purposefulness, he said, 'Don't ever let me run across you again, or you'll find that there is always a price to pay, and it just might amuse me to see that you pay it!'

Even now, ten years later, the memory of those ruthless words sent a shiver across Tegan's skin, as did the remembered pain of that gratuitous insult. How young and naïve she'd been, and how silly. Silly enough to have jeopardised her whole future, just because she couldn't bring herself to say no to a man who said he needed her. If it hadn't been for her mother's intervention she'd probably have been persuaded by Sam's calm assumption that she was going to marry him into doing just that, and then they'd both have been bitterly unhappy.

Poor Sam. After that fiasco he had gone on expanding his software empire; there had been a marriage, but it had been brief. Now he lived in America, known the world over for his brilliance in his chosen field.

Tegan still remembered the hero-worship in his voice when he'd talked about Kieran Sinclair, the man who had befriended him when he was a lonely, unhappy child imprisoned by his physical disabilities and his parents' conviction that he would never achieve anything, the man whose faith in him had set him on the road to wealth and whatever independence he now possessed.

And she would always remember Kieran Sinclair's barely restrained fury, the bitter, savage contempt that still marked her soul. He hadn't needed to be so brutal. One glance should have told him that Tegan was unsophisticated and self-centred rather than conniving and greedy.

Clearly, she decided with an acid smile, the past years hadn't softened him in the least.

He had packed a lot into them, working in London for several years before coming back to New Zealand to take over a more or less moribund little finance company owned by his uncles and whipping it into a successful merchant bank, the biggest in the country and growing internationally. His photograph appeared regularly in the newspaper beside laudatory, respectful articles. He must be about thirty-five now, young for such status, but Tegan wasn't surprised.

A reluctant, resentful fascination might mean that she read everything that appeared about him, but she hadn't forgotten a second of that terrifying interview. His formidable, implacable strength of purpose had made such an impression that if she closed her eyes she could still see his face, still hear every intonation of the deep, crisp voice.

She pushed her fingers through hair so dark a red it was usually taken for black until the sun struck fire from the thick mass of it. It was useless to brood over past humiliations; she had work to do.

Five minutes later the buzzer rang. Smiling wryly, Tegan reached out a long-fingered hand and lifted the receiver. 'Yep?'

Her usually calm partner sounded harried. 'We have to talk. Can you come in here? I'm waiting for a call from El Amir.'

They had high hopes of being commissioned to decorate a new palace in the tiny Middle East emirate, so there was no way they could afford to miss the call. With the lithe, athletic stride that came from long legs and lots of tennis, Tegan went into Blair's office. Her partner looked up, a frown pinching her brows together. 'I suppose Alana told you what happened?'

'Yes. With considerable huff and puff. Not that I blame her; he was less than tactful.'

Blair shrugged. 'He didn't get where he is by being tactful to interior decorators; we're totally small fry to him.' She looked speculatively at Tegan.

Tegan's stomach dropped in swift, shaming panic. 'Ten years ago he made it quite clear that he never wanted to set eyes on me again.'

Blair sighed. 'Of all the people to fall foul of...'

'I didn't try to do it, believe me! Oh, what a mess! But I was certain Alana could pull it off.'

'So was I. She should have been able to, of course; she just tried too hard. She wanted to impress him personally, and that's fatal. But you're going to have to give it a go.' Blair fiddled with her pen. 'I don't have to tell you we need the money, Tegan.'

'No.' For a moment they both sat in gloomy silence, contemplating their situation. The stockmarket crash had cut their income in half, and struggling back was difficult. Before that they had been offered far more work than they could handle. Now they had to go out and look for it. It was the part of the business neither of them found particularly enjoyable, but in spite of their best efforts the business was only just paying its way.

'I know you really enjoy helping the people in the state housing scheme, but it doesn't bring any money in,' Blair continued. 'We have to subsidise it with nice, fat contracts from nice, rich people.'

'I know,' Tegan said, dragging her mind back from the ominous figures on their latest bank statement. Her clients in the state housing scheme were mostly young, with no money to squander, and Blair was perfectly correct—it was a labour of love. Resigned to the inevitable, Tegan set her mind to planning. 'Alana should suit the Sheridans; with any luck she'll do very well for them, as they're as desperately trendy as she is. I'll take her over and introduce her this afternoon—I'll tell them she's our expert on modern furnishings, and drop in a few items from that extremely glowing c.v. of hers. No need to tell him it's five years since she worked as a professional. Then I'll get straight on to drafting out a scheme for Kieran Sinclair's place. At least Alana's got all the data. You'll have to front for me, though, because unless he's changed enormously in the last few years he'd like nothing better than to throw me off the property. He despises me.'

'I wonder why?' Blair's sleepy green eyes hid a very shrewd brain. 'And don't tell me it's because Sam

thingy fell in love with you and you couldn't recipro-
cate. That happens all the time.'

Tegan shrugged. 'He thought I was a gold-digger.'

'Wonderful old-fashioned turn of phrase.' Blair
spoke in a vague voice but the look she turned on to her
friend was sharp. 'He must know you're not, otherwise
you'd have married Sam and cheated on him. Ah, well,
it doesn't matter; it's all water under the bridge. Trust
malignant fate to make it happen now, when I'm struggling with the emir's palace. You should have dealt with
Sinclair in the first place instead of Alana, but, as you
say, we couldn't risk anything that might put him off.
Now we have to. Do you think he doesn't know you're
a partner in Decorators Inc?'

Tegan sighed, lifting her brows. 'I don't presume to
be able to read his mind. If the way he carried on after
I broke my engagement to Sam was any indication, he'd
have cut off his right hand rather than contact a firm
with me as one of the principals. Although that might
be putting too much emphasis on what happened then.
Perhaps he doesn't even remember me.'

'But you don't believe that.'

Tegan's voice was ironic. 'No. He didn't strike me as
a man who'd forget grudges.'

'Then we'll just have to lay a little smokescreen,' Blair
said crisply. 'You have a skill amounting damned near
to genius for bringing old houses back to life, so the old
Raintree place should be a perfect vehicle for your tal-
ents. I wonder why Sinclair bought it, when he must
know he could have built himself a mansion with a sea
view for considerably less money?'

'What sort of smokescreen?' Tegan asked suspi-
ciously.

Blair gave her a conspiratorial smile. 'Kieran Sinclair's heading overseas—some bankers' conference in Switzerland, and then he's going on somewhere else—skiing, if he's got any sense, the lucky devil. He'll be away for a couple of months.'

'How do you know all this?'

'His secretary rang me a few minutes ago and told me. He expects me to take over the job. I'm to organise a presentation within a week and get it to him, then he'll decide whether or not to use us.' Her long fingers fidgeted with a slim pen. After a moment she said, 'Damn the man; why couldn't he have wanted a madly modern interior? Come to that, why couldn't Alana have worked out that a man who paid several millions for a run-down old classic in Remuera wouldn't want it converted into a yuppie's dream? I hope she turns out all right.'

Tegan nodded. They had hired Alana because she had excellent, if elderly credentials, and because she was prepared to work hard. Neither admitted that one of the reasons she got the position was her need to re-establish herself after a traumatic divorce had left her with no money and two children to support.

'What's Kieran Sinclair like?' Blair asked suddenly. 'I mean, from a reasonably sophisticated woman's point of view, as opposed to a terrified, traumatised girl's.'

Tegan pulled a face. 'He's old money. According to an interview I read he's a complex, fascinating man. He's certainly loyal; if he could have, he'd have forced me to marry Sam!'

'So we need to come up with a complex, fascinating scheme, firmly rooted in tradition. Just up your alley.'

'Yes,' Tegan said without enthusiasm.

Blair gave a sympathetic smile. 'With any luck you won't even have to meet the man. Is he the sort to hover over the job, checking everything the tradesmen do?'

'No. He's the sort to insist that whoever does the checking does it well. He demands the best, but I doubt whether he personally will be breathing down our necks to make sure we deliver. From what I've read, he delegates well; it's part of the reason for his success.'

'That should make things much easier. You'll just have to keep out of the way.'

Tegan grinned sardonically. 'Oh, yes, I can just see it. We'll be playing hide-and-seek around the site for weeks. Ah, well, I'd better start planning, I suppose. When do you leave for El Amir?'

'Ten days.'

It had been an immense feather in their cap to be asked to put in a bid for the emir's palace. They owed the chance to Blair, who had met the emir's son a year ago when he was buying racehorses in the Waikato, and impressed him enough for him to recall her name. If they were commissioned to do the palace they'd have cracked the international market. From then on the sky would be their limit, but until that happened they couldn't afford to let a job of any size go.

'I just hope Kieran Sinclair doesn't find out it's my baby,' Tegan said gloomily.

Blair lifted her brows. 'He's a businessman; he's not going to lose money breaking a contract just because you once refused to marry a friend of his. Tegan, Raintree House is going to be one of *the* places to go in Auckland. Kieran Sinclair has connections to everyone who's anyone; if we do a good job for him it won't be such a disaster if we lose the emir's palace.'

Tegan opened her mouth but Blair was looking at her with naked appeal, and after a moment Tegan sighed. She owed the woman opposite her a lot. It was Blair who had talked her father into lending them the money to start up their business five years ago, but their friendship had begun at boarding school, where they had been the two tallest pupils. Together they had faced down tormenters and their own insecurities.

They complemented each other. While both had artistic flair and panache, Blair's tendency to drama and opulence needed the balance of Tegan's more level outlook. When it came to old houses, and people who wanted a miraculous mixture of old and new, Tegan was the expert.

'Of course you're right,' she said on an exhaled breath. 'I'll get on to it straight away.'

'You'll love it.' Blair was bracing. 'You've been dying to get your hands on Raintree House for years.'

Tegan's generous mouth pulled into a grimace. 'I've often peered in through the gates and wondered what it was like behind that amazing jungle. It's a shame such a magnificent old place was let go to rack and ruin. I wonder if he'll change the name to Sinclair House?'

Two acres of land, however neglected, in the heart of Remuera, one of Auckland's most expensive suburbs, had cost Kieran Sinclair a packet. It was going to cost even more to bring the huge house back to anything like liveable-in order. The last Raintree had been an unmarried daughter who had allowed it to moulder quietly about her for fifty years.

'Who knows?' Blair gestured expansively. 'It's all yours. Incidentally, who was the handsome man I saw you with at the Mercury Theatre last night? I thought you were going out with Ray Turner? I never know from one day to the next who you're going to have falling over themselves to lay their hearts at your cold, hard feet for you to spurn.'

'Oh, rubbish! I don't spurn any of them.'

'Stop avoiding the issue. Who was he, and what happened to the masterful Ray?'

Tegan knew when she had her back to the wall. 'You're so nosy! He wanted to get married.'

'Of course he wanted to get married. I don't know how you do it! Other women complain because their boyfriends want affairs, but not you—all yours want to marry you.'

'You make me sound like a stamp collector.'

'Oh, I know you don't want them to fall in love with you, but they do. Why don't you marry one of them and put the rest out of their misery?'

'I've never met a man who could make me feel that marriage was better than being single.' It was Tegan's stock reply, one she used whenever anyone asked that question. It was the truth, too, but only a part of it.

She had long ago given up protesting that she was no *femme fatale*, and she certainly had no intention of revealing even to Blair that the men in her life were sent on their way when they started to talk marriage, or sex, or even commitment.

'So who,' Blair asked relentlessly, 'was last night's cavalier, and how long has he been on the scene?'

Tegan sighed ostentatiously. 'He's called Peter Hampshire, I've been out with him a couple of times in the last fortnight, and he is not a cavalier.'

'He wants to be your lover. Does he realise that he's not going to get there?'

Tegan hooded her eyes and thinned her mouth, wishing, not for the first time, that she didn't work with a woman who had known her since she was twelve.

Totally unimpressed, Blair grinned. 'Well, does he?'

'Of course he does. I told him I wasn't in the market for an affair, and he said he's not either.'

'And you believed him? Honestly, Tegan, sometimes I don't think you've learnt anything. OK, OK, I'm not going to say any more, but don't come wailing to me when you discover that he's been lusting after your body all the time you thought you were having a nice easy friendship. Men don't know what platonic means.'

To the sound of her friend's laughter, Tegan pulled a hideous face and left her.

'OK, Geoff, that's fine; I take your point about the panelling. I agree, and I'll get it organised.'

With a smile at the architect Tegan turned to walk out of the front door, just as a gleaming olive-green and silver Jaguar purred to a halt at the bottom of the steps.

Her heart performed a complicated manoeuvre in her chest. With dilated eyes she watched as the driver killed the engine and got out of the car. My God, she had forgotten how big Kieran Sinclair was!

He hadn't seen her; he was looking across at what had once been, and was going to be again, a tennis court. His profile was a beautiful but forbidding line. Fire sizzled across Tegan's nerve-ends as she registered the high forehead, a slashing straight nose that gave him the air of haughty arrogance he had used to intimidate Alana, a wide, uncompromising but beautifully chiselled mouth, and a chin and jawline that indicated he was not in the habit of making compromises.

Just the way Kieran Sinclair carried his head told the world that here was a man who expected the world to adjust to him.

Tegan's breath stopped in her throat. This was what she had been dreading for the last four weeks, ever since she'd drawn up the scheme for Kieran Sinclair. Fortunately he had liked it, and everything had gone along smoothly since then. He wasn't supposed to be back from his overseas trip for weeks yet, so what the hell was he doing here now? Clearly her luck had run out.

Panic clutched her; she froze, hoping against hope that he would go over to where the tennis court was being refurbished so she could get away. But of course she couldn't just turn tail and flee. Blair wasn't going to be back from El Amir for at least a week, so it was up to Tegan to deal with him.

He turned and saw her. For a moment they both stood perfectly still, staring at each other. Then he started purposefully up to the house. As he came towards her something strange and completely untoward happened to Tegan's spine. For a second she felt as though she'd been subjected to some kind of psychic assault, but the alarming sensations that rioted through her were more physical than spiritual.

Dressed in a dark business suit that bore the unmistakable stamp of excellent tailoring, Kieran held her imprisoned by an icy aquamarine gaze. But it was not the clothes, or even the magnificently masculine framework and colouring of his face and body, that made him so daunting.

It was the instant recognition that swamped Tegan's thinking process, as though she knew him intimately, soul to soul, as though she had been waiting for him for aeons. *This is the man, and you are the woman.*

So powerful was the shattering moment of empathy that she couldn't drag her gaze away from him, so she saw the exact moment when he recognised her.

'Tegan Jones,' he said through his teeth. 'I wondered when you were going to crawl out of the woodwork.'

'Mr Sinclair,' she responded numbly, forcing her outstretched hand to stop trembling.

Amazingly, his fingers closed over hers in a brief handshake. Her breath tightened in her throat. She felt—*claimed*, she thought dazedly. Taken over. Conquered. A bolt of lightning travelled up her arm and engulfed her while she looked up helplessly.

Instantly his face hardened into lines of cold, clear contempt and he dropped her hand with deliberate scorn. 'What the hell are you doing here? Looking for another rich man to fleece?' His voice was deep and measured, and he was watching her with crystal flames in those brilliant blue-green eyes.

Swift and primal, sensation raced through her. She would not lie to him. 'I'm supervising the decorating of your house,' she told him quietly, ignoring his rudeness and contempt.

Black brows drew together. 'Like hell you are! Where's the Cartwright woman? I gave the contract to her.'

'Yes, you did, but she's overseas at the moment——'

'I don't care if she's in Timbuktu—she took on this job and she's going to see it through. I don't want you anywhere near this place.' Close up, the severe, unqualified beauty of his features was breathtaking. But in spite of the dense, exotic sea-green eyes his expression was implacable, and nothing, Tegan thought despairingly, would ever soften the uncompromising mouth.

Antagonism flared to life in her, sharpening her golden gaze into narrowed brilliance. 'For your information, I'm the other half of Decorators Inc. I'm as qualified as Blair to supervise your house. If you don't want me you'll have to make do with Alana Richmond,' she said curtly.

'I see.' He smiled, a hard-edged challenge that paradoxically highlighted a sudden smouldering sensuality. 'I don't want her either. She's utterly useless, as useless as I'm sure you are. Mrs Cartwright has a singularly inept understanding of character if she thinks that she's going to get away with fobbing you off on to me. The moment you get back to your office you'd better fax or ring her and tell her to get back here as soon as she can, or lose the job.'

Tegan's long neck ached, but she refused to back down. 'Blair won't be back for a week,' she said.

'The contract specifies that she work on Raintree House. She can damned well come back from wherever she is and do it.'

Tegan took a deep breath, willing it to flow smoothly into her lungs. 'Mr Sinclair, you liked the original presentation. Why don't you go in and see what's been done before you make any decision? I don't think you'll be disappointed.'

'Disappointment,' he said in far too even a voice, 'is not what I feel, believe me. I do not want you working on my house. I don't think I can make it any clearer than that.'

'Very well.' The words were clipped and icy. 'I'll send Alana out to deal with it, then. Goodbye.'

'You needn't,' he said harshly, 'bother sending anyone out. I am terminating the contract as of now. Oh, and before you go running off to the lawyer, read it through. It's watertight. Blair Cartwright or nobody. So don't expect to get another cent out of me. I can stand the expense of a lawsuit much better than you can.'

Appalled, Tegan said, 'Mr Sinclair——'

'Get off my property.' He spoke without any inflexion at all, in the same voice that he had used to tear her to shreds ten years before.

The fear and humiliation she had felt then smirched her again. 'Very well, then,' she said as calmly as she could, and turned and walked away to where her car was parked among the tradesmen's vans and trucks, her heart hammering so loudly that she couldn't hear the noise of their tools above it.

Alana had been right. Only 'arrogant swine' didn't describe him adequately. Surreptitiously she wiped the palms of her hands on her trousers as she risked a swift, unobtrusive glance across at him. He was still standing on the steps watching her, the sun turning his hair into a tawny aureole around his proudly poised head.

Ironic, when it would be hard to find a man less like a saint!

Back at the office she tried to ring Blair in her hotel at El Amir. There was no answer so she faxed a message through, then worked determinedly on another presentation until five, ignoring her churning stomach and tension headache. She had to go home then because she was going out to a barbecue with Peter Hampshire.

It was the last thing she wanted to do. God, she'd blown it completely! Blair would be shattered—damn Kieran Sinclair, picking over old quarrels like a vulture, behaving—yes, Alana was right, behaving like some fantasy lord of the manor!

Tegan's firm, square little chin angled defiantly. No, she wouldn't gnaw over the whole savage incident like a dog with a bone. Better by far to work out how she was going to make the most of the evening. Although this was a barbecue she was going to, it was also a business occasion; Peter's boss was giving it for colleagues and business associates, and she had learned over the years that any social occasion could be turned to good use.

It was the part of her career she liked least, this inconspicuous, unaggressive touting for business. However, as Blair said, who also disliked it but managed to carry it off with her usual panache, it had to be done. Businesses like theirs relied on word of mouth, on casual gossip, on personal recommendations, but mainly on the personal appeal of the decorators, to initiate the first contact. So they had to go out and be recognised, know who was who; this evening would be work.

It promised to end unpleasantly, too. Tegan was going to have to tell Peter, if not tonight then fairly soon, that she wasn't interested in any closer relationship than friendship. She wasn't looking forward to the conversation. What made it exasperating was that when he had first asked her out he had sworn that friendship was all he wanted from her. He was, he'd said, his handsome face completely sincere, tired of affairs that went nowhere. He wanted a pleasant, relaxed association that put no pressure on either of them.

And she'd fallen for probably the oldest line in the book! During the last couple of weeks it had become ever more apparent that his idea of friendship had nothing in common with hers, and, although he might not feel pressured, *she* certainly was by the expectations and the possessiveness he was no longer trying to hide.

An hour later she was almost ready in a voile wrap skirt of clear gold, chosen because it was light and pretty, and would stand up to energetic dancing as well as the heat and humidity of an Auckland summer night. It was topped with a cropped voile shirt in warm turquoise. She tied the ends of the shirt together under her breasts, revealing a pale triangle of midriff. The outfit wasn't too *outré*, but people would remember her, which was the object of the exercise.

'Mind you,' she said to her reflection, 'most people remember a woman who is almost six feet tall, anyway! All I need to do is arrive!'

But she enjoyed wearing dramatic clothes. It had taken her a few years to lose the last of her adolescent horror at calling attention to herself, but she had managed it.

The sound of the clock chimes recalled her attention. Hastily she clipped on a pair of her trademark large earrings, these ones barbaric in mingled shades of turquoise and gold, and slid her long, elegant feet into high-heeled sandals in soft turquoise leather. As she blended smoky teal eyeshadow with ivory highlighter on to her eyelids, Tegan admitted with wry self-derision that she was dressing up more than she would normally for a barbecue. A carry-over from that intimidating meeting with Kieran Sinclair, no doubt.

Peter was oddly strung up, his pleasant face for once not set in lines of laughter.

'What's the matter?' Tegan asked, catching her breath as he ran a red light.

'Nothing. Nothing at all.' His fingers drummed on the wheel. 'It should be a good evening. The boss has pulled out all the stops tonight; the caterers are spit-roasting a suckling pig, and we're drinking the second-best champagne. Of course, apart from being informed that I'm on duty I'm not in his confidence, but clearly he wants to impress someone. Incidentally, that was bad news about El Amir, wasn't it? I suppose it means your firm won't be decorating a palace after all, unless the new ruler wants it.'

'What?'

'Didn't you hear the news? There's been a revolution there, and the old ruler's fled the country.'

'Oh, God.' The unanswered telephone in the hotel room suddenly assumed new and ominous significance. 'Blair's over there now,' Tegan said in a flat little voice, hideous images from various television programmes dancing in front of her eyes.

'Is she? Well, not to worry; the reports said there have been no reports of casualties, and it seems foreigners are not in any danger at all. No doubt you'll hear from her tomorrow.'

'We should go back,' she said, her forehead wrinkling as she tried to assess the implications. 'I'll have to ring Gerald to see whether he's heard from her.'

'Gerald? Oh, yes, her husband.' Peter frowned. 'We'll be late if we go back, and that won't look too good for me. One thing old Piper is hot on is punctuality. Look, why don't you ask him if you can use his phone when we get there?'

'Yes. Yes, all right, I'll do that.'

Rodney Piper and his wife lived in a large, somewhat over-decorated house on the slopes of One Tree
Hill, and they were quite happy to let Tegan ring Gerald
from the telephone in the hall. However, there was no
answer.

'No luck?'

Peter's harassed query brought her head around. 'No,
which must be a good sign, because if there was any
danger at all Gerald would be burning the lines between here and every contact he has.' She slid her hand
around his arm, smiling into his face. 'Cheer up.'

'It's easy enough for you to say,' he muttered fret-
fully. 'Tegan——'

Tegan raised her straight black brows, but before she
could ask him what was going on there was a burst of
laughter from outside, and his expression altered.
'Come on, hurry up; we'd better get out there.'

It was all set to be a fairly typical occasion, an uneasy hybrid between business and pleasure. Tegan did
what she always did—pretended that it was a play—and
with the aid of her lively imagination kept creeping
boredom at bay——

Until she looked across the elegant pool, carefully
landscaped to resemble a bush waterhole, and saw the
last red rays of the sun strike old gold sparks from
Kieran Sinclair's head. He was dressed impeccably in
summer style, casual yet well tailored, and, above all in
this warm northern climate, cool. Again his height and
his size struck her, but although they added to his powerful presence its most potent source came from within
him; his character was the basis of his very male authority.

Tegan's boredom vanished, to be replaced by borderline panic. As though enchanted by some dark magician's spell, she watched him smile at the woman with him, and was dismayingly conscious of a clutch of sensation in the pit of her stomach.

She knew what it was, of course. Attraction, the subtle tumult in the blood that made fools of all men and women. Well, she had squashed it before, and she'd do it again. She wasn't going to end up the besotted slave of a purely chemical reaction.

One of the disadvantages of her height was its conspicuousness; she looked away, but in a very short time she felt the unnerving tension under her skin that denoted a steady stare. Ignoring it, she smiled at Peter, who had been busily circulating until a couple of minutes before.

'I think I'll slip inside and see if I can raise Gerald again,' she said.

He looked cross but said immediately, 'I'll come with you.'

'No, don't bother, I know you're on duty.'

He drained his glass and took her hand. 'Darling girl, it's no bother, as you well know.'

The significant look that accompanied his words produced a silent sigh. Why, oh, why couldn't men and women just be friends? She liked Peter very much, but that was all. Although she had enjoyed their outings together, the end was definitely approaching.

She avoided the area where Kieran was holding court, but even so she breathed more lightly when she was out of his sight. There was still no answer from Gerald.

'Perhaps he's out, and hasn't heard,' she said, putting the receiver back.

'Quite possibly.' Expertly Peter twirled her around and caught her close to him. One hand slid across her waist at the back, stroking the fine skin.

'Peter,' she said warningly.

'Tegan.' He was mocking her, but his voice was thick. 'Tegan,' he said again. 'You must know how I feel about you.'

A firm grip on his upper arms held him a little away. 'I told you,' she reminded him, 'that I wasn't in the market for an affair.'

'Yes. It was clever of you, because of course that's what I wanted at first, but I want more than that now.' Ignoring the swift, decisive shake of her head, he went on urgently, 'I know it's too soon, I know you said you wouldn't change your mind, but I can't keep our bargain any longer. I love you. I want to marry you. Tegan, I'll promise you anything you want; you can have——'

'Shh.' The hairs on the back of her neck stirred. She pulled free and looked past him, but there was no one there. 'I thought I heard someone,' she said. 'Peter, we can't talk here. Wait until later.'

Why did he have to choose tonight, of all nights, when she was strung up worrying about both Blair and that nasty little scene with Kieran Sinclair?

Oddly self-conscious as she walked out into the lazy warmth of the evening, she looked around, and of course the first person her eyes fell on was Kieran, standing beside Peter's boss a few feet away. Tegan's eyes met a glance the colour of the tropical lagoons, the colour of summer, and something inside her tightened unbearably.

'No reply?' asked Rodney Piper, frowning fractionally at Peter.

'No.' Tegan managed to smile. 'I think it's probably a good sign. Gerald would certainly be ringing every contact he has if there was anything to worry about.'

'Of course he would.' Rodney turned. 'Now, have you met Kieran Sinclair? Kieran, this is Tegan——'

'Tegan and I have met.'

How did he manage to smile when his eyes and mouth were so hard and unrelenting?

'Then, if you don't mind, I'll leave you together while Peter and I make sure everyone's got a drink.'

And, collecting a hangdog Peter, he bustled off, leaving an oddly taut silence behind him.

'You're looking very attractive tonight. Ivory dusted with gold—and that's just your skin.' Kieran's voice was lazy, almost amused.

Tegan looked up, and immediately stepped back. He was still smiling, but there was no warmth in the teal-blue gaze that made a slow, deliberate inspection of her body before lingering speculatively on the width of satin flesh between her top and the waistband of her skirt.

Other men had looked her over, but this offensive survey had nothing of their essentially admiring appreciation; Kieran looked as though he was assessing her for her sexual potential, as though she were a slave in the market place and his sole reason for being there was to buy a concubine.

Tegan was not particularly modest. She knew she had a good figure, that it was strong and supple and attractive to men, and normally she didn't mind them enjoying it. But the look in Kieran Sinclair's eyes brought her defensive instincts slamming into action.

CHAPTER TWO

KIERAN stared with all the arrogance of his wild Celtic ancestors as they rode with bloody weapons across Europe, conquering and plundering, carrying with them their ferocious religion and their exquisite art. Well, Tegan too was descended from those fighting tribesmen. Her dark brows lifted; she sent him a resentful glare.

A smile, worldly and experienced, quirked his mouth. Outraged, humiliated by the fact that she could feel that smouldering gaze right through to her bones, Tegan's eyes snapped golden fire. Some secret, tender, inner part of her soul had been violated, but in subtle, un-mistakable ways her body was responding to that insulting appraisal.

She turned away sharply, despising herself, furious with him.

'Have you been trying to ring Blair Cartwright?' he asked.

With intense reluctance she said, 'Yes, I tried several times today, but I couldn't get her. And her husband's not at home.' Her teeth clenched a moment before she said unwillingly, 'I hope she's all right.'

'Of course she is. The trouble in El Amir is a purely internal affair. The emir was too radical, so he's been demoted and one of his more conservative cousins will take over.'

'How do you know?'

He shrugged slightly. 'In my business it pays to keep up with world affairs. El Amir has been ripe for trouble for some time; anyone with any foresight at all could have told there was going to be turmoil there soon. My contacts in the area have been warning me to be wary of the place for the last five years.'

Against her will Tegan was intrigued. She said, 'I should keep up with things, but I don't, I'm afraid.'

'Too busy reading *House and Garden*, I suppose,' he said, investing the words with the flavour of a taunt. 'Tell me, what persuaded you to be an interior decorator?'

For a moment Tegan toyed with the idea of suggesting he go to hell and take his patronising questions with him, but she was able to overcome the reckless impulse. It was necessary to keep on his right side because if his summing-up of the situation in El Amir was correct, and it probably was, the emir's palace was almost certainly a lost cause.

'My parents let me design my own room when I was sixteen,' she told him coolly. 'Blair was my best friend at boarding school, and she came to stay one holiday. She coaxed her parents into letting us do hers. We really enjoyed doing it, and the room got so many compliments that we decided that's what we'd do when we left school. So Blair took a degree in fine arts while I did one in business administration. After a couple of years gaining experience we set up in business together.'

'You spent time overseas, I believe.'

Now, how did he know that? She had fled overseas after the débâcle of Sam Hoskings. 'Yes. A year in London, and one in California.'

'That must have been useful,' he said, his voice remote.

Tegan looked up sharply, but he was watching someone else with narrowed, intent eyes. When she turned her head to see who it was, an odd pang gripped her. His gaze was fixed on a very beautiful woman who was laughing with another man, her lashes lowered as she blatantly flirted with him.

Almost instantly Kieran Sinclair looked down at Tegan again, but there was for a moment a bleak acceptance in his expression that made her feel a sudden, intensely reluctant sympathy.

'So you get fulfilment from following all the latest trends in design,' he said, and the mockery was back in his voice.

She shrugged, angry because he watched the movement of her shoulders, his glance lingering far too intimately on the pale gold skin. He was deliberately trying to provoke her; she didn't believe that he was normally so crass.

Defiantly, she let her eyes wander over him with the same insulting scrutiny he had subjected her to. It backfired. He was physically perfect. Stunningly handsome men were not as common as attractive women, so when one came into view he tended to make a bigger impact.

But, even as she tried to rationalise his effect on her away, Tegan knew that it was not just his physical perfection that so affected her. Put simply, Kieran Sinclair had a potent, masculine authority that made him stand out even in that assembly of rich and powerful men.

Tegan's voice was a little unsteady as she countered, 'What made you decide to be a merchant banker?'

He sent her a look of purest, coldest crystal, so sharp that it pierced through her armour of self-possession and almost wrung a soft cry of protest from her.

'You could say it was an ambition I'd long cherished,' he said aloofly. 'I wasn't very old when I realised that money gives you choices, options that are denied those who don't have it.' His tone forbade further enquiry.

Shaken more by that fierce raptor's glance than his words, Tegan didn't pursue the subject. Instead she asked, 'Do you like your job?'

'Yes. I enjoy working on projects that are going to help the country, that show initiative and flair and the promise of growth. I like helping people who are creative and forward-thinking, who are prepared to work hard to make their ambitions come true.'

And, Tegan supplied silently, you like power.

'Darling,' Peter said into her ear, 'I'm sorry I had to desert you.' He slid a possessive arm around her shoulders, and the smile he directed at Kieran Sinclair was a mixture of apology and challenge.

Furious with him, Tegan nevertheless bristled at the knowledgeable amusement that surfaced a moment in the aquamarine depths of the taller man's eyes. 'Not to worry,' he said calmly.

They were interrupted by Rodney Piper, escorting someone he wanted to introduce to the star of his party. With great thankfulness Tegan allowed Peter to steer her away.

Her gratitude didn't last, however, for Peter was in a belligerent mood. 'I didn't like the way he was looking at you,' he said truculently, snagging a drink for them both. 'He's a big bad wolf, is Kieran Sinclair. Women throw themselves at him all the time, and he enjoys the ones he wants and then goes on to the next. He's notorious for it.'

'He seems to be rather interested in the pretty woman in the slinky gold outfit.'

Peter gave a snort of laughter. 'That's his sister, the beauteous and bitchy Andrea. I must say we're profoundly honoured to have her here. She doesn't usually bother with dreary business affairs. She's more the glitz-and-glamour type.'

Horrified by the sudden surge of relief that washed through her, Tegan said, 'She's very lovely.'

'She is also,' Peter muttered softly in her ear, 'a truly decadent lady. Apparently she's just done an Odyssey course, or treatment, or whatever it is. Although I've never heard they hold ones for nymphomania.'

Sympathy for both the woman and her brother bridled Tegan's response. But as she tried to pull away Kieran Sinclair looked across. His gaze came to rest on Peter who chose that moment to nuzzle the junction of her neck and shoulder. Tegan jerked away but couldn't stop colour heating her cheeks. Shame and embarrassment at gossiping about him curdled inside her. As though he recognised her emotions his black brows lifted and a hard little smile curled his beautifully moulded, uncompromising mouth.

Almost flinching, Tegan looked away, but the impact of that scornful glance stayed like a stain on her skin.

Fortunately her gaze was caught by the sight of Rodney Piper stooping over the huge, up-market, expensive barbecue where the glistening suckling pig was being basted. 'I didn't realise your boss took such an interest in the actual cooking on these occasions,' she said, aware that she was babbling but unable to think of anything else to say.

Laughing, Peter hugged her, then neglected to take his arm away. 'He's just a backyard griller at heart. I suspect he's always sorry he has to hand the cooking over to the professionals, because he certainly likes to keep an eye on them.'

They were joined by another couple, and to Tegan's hidden relief conversation became general. The evening wore on. She managed to enjoy herself, even though she was irritated by Peter's overtly proprietorial air, and nagged by the fear that Blair might be in trouble.

After the superb barbecue food had been given due appreciation music drifted from inside the house, lilting, beguiling, perfect for dancing. Lured by it, people began to move into the big leisure-room off the terrace. Others stood around in small groups, both inside the house and around the pool, talking and laughing and flirting. All seemed to be enjoying themselves immensely. Looking around through a barrier of alienation, Tegan wondered why on earth she was there with people she didn't care about and never wanted to see again, when she wanted to be at home finding out whether Blair was safe or not.

'Let's dance,' Peter muttered into her ear. 'I've been waiting all evening to hold you.'

But before they had a chance to move Rodney Piper came up. 'Peter, how about looking after Ben Thompson's daughter?' he suggested, smiling perfunctorily at Tegan. 'She's standing by herself at the moment. Young thing like that, she's bound to feel upset.'

'Damn,' Peter said beneath his breath, but he was enough of a corporation man to know an order when he heard one, and to obey it. He smiled at Tegan. 'You'll be OK, won't you?'

Tegan was rather relieved than otherwise. In his present mood dancing with Peter wasn't likely to be relaxing or pleasant. 'Yes, of course.'

As soon as they had gone she sat down on a secluded seat beneath a pergola draped with the sweet white flowers of summer jasmine, and prepared to enjoy a few moments of peace.

Inevitably, her glance was captured by the intense beauty of Kieran Sinclair's countenance. He was talking to three other men, all of them older than he was, all listening respectfully, and in spite of the mundane occasion he looked like some golden god of old, a sculptor's vision rendered into flesh, with all the perils of such a visitation open and apparent in his features.

Viewed objectively, of course, he couldn't be as dangerous as he seemed. He was just a man, albeit a big, powerfully elegant, particularly handsome one. But some atavistic instinct normally buried deep in Tegan's unconscious had immediately recognised him to be an intrinsic threat to her peace of mind.

He posed an elemental problem—that of controlling the incandescent, wildfire attraction he roused in her. But she was confident of her ability to do that. What made her afraid was that in some strange, fundamental way, merely by being the man he was, he challenged all that was female in her, daring her to prove her femininity.

Of course, being a sensible, practical person, she told herself there was no way she was going to accept that primitive dare. She would be at too much of a disadvantage. Kieran kept the complexities of his personality well hidden. His cryptic, compelling aura hinted of other qualities, some very much at variance with the autocratic self-possession and the sophistication that struck her so forcibly each time she saw him.

Ivory dusted with gold... She could still hear his deep, textured voice as he said the words, the lick of arousal he hadn't been able to hide. And, heaven help her, even recalling it aroused a slow burn throughout her body.

'Would you like to dance?'

It was as though her thoughts had summoned him. He blocked out the rest of the world, large, forbidding, and perilously attractive.

Tegan didn't say no, which was what intuition was suggesting forcefully would be her safest course. But it was with the greatest reluctance that she went beside him through the softly humid darkness into the big, dimly lit party room.

Without speaking, he took her into his arms. He danced with an underlying sensuality that was unsettling, ignoring completely the interested glances he was getting from everyone else in the room. It still didn't seem fair that a tall man was always admired, whereas a tall woman was often ignored; Tegan had suffered many times as a wallflower at school dances during the years when no boy of her age was tall enough to see over her shoulder.

Just another example of the double standard, she thought moodily. A man built like him shouldn't be able to dance gracefully either, but Kieran moved with a collected suppleness that roused something quick and unrestrained inside her, a pang of response she couldn't stifle.

Excitement scorched along her nerves, transformed her eyes to pure gold spangles in her vivid face, but Tegan reined in the tide of awareness that could easily wash her into the dark depths of desire. She had to be sensible. It would be stupidly reckless to court disaster, and that was what she would be doing if she gave in to this unsupported, antagonistic attraction.

It was difficult, but for most of the time she spent in his arms she was able to sublimate her response by concentrating on the music and the pleasure of dancing with Kieran. Then the tape changed, the music drifted into something smoky and sensual, and his arms tightened as he looked down into her face, his features set, half-closed sea-coloured eyes glittering and strangely intent.

The hand about hers was cool and hard. His other hand slid down her back and opened across the smooth skin at her waist. Tegan thought she might suffocate, her heart beat so high in her throat, but she kept her eyes straight ahead, staring at his perfectly cut lips, the strong statement of jaw and chin, and the high, slashing line of his cheekbones.

Slowly, painfully, she achieved some sort of self-control. But she didn't dare trust her voice, so she followed his lead and was silent. His arm across her back was firm but not too heavy, and soon she tamped down that brutal awareness. The moving couples around them were reflected in the topaz mirrors of her eyes while her whole mind and body were focused on the man who held her with such calm authority.

Sudden laughter across the room broke into Tegan's trance. Turning her face so she could focus on the source, she realised that it was his sister, Andrea. Flushed and a little unsteady on her heels, she was leaning against a man Tegan didn't know. His hand came up to rest on her shoulder, and he squeezed. It was a small caress, but the intimacy was blatant.

Every muscle in Kieran Sinclair's big body locked taut. For a moment Tegan was assailed by a menace so obvious that her heart stopped. Then she felt him relax, gradually, deliberately.

She tilted her head—it was, she thought vaguely, almost the first time she had actually had to do that to be able to look into a man's face. He was staring across at the other side of the room, and his eyes were the coldest she had ever seen—opaque and enigmatic as turquoise.

'Your sister is enjoying herself,' she said, unconsciously turning the words into a challenge.

'Yes.' His mouth barely moved. Then he dragged his gaze away and looked down into Tegan's still, waiting face. Banked sensuality flared suddenly into life as he smiled.

Tegan actually pulled back, but his arms tightened about her, imprisoning her. With the casual strength of a man hugging a child he forced her against the lean hardness of his body, overcoming her instinctive rigidity with insulting ease. 'Relax,' he murmured into her ear. 'I'm not going to attack you.'

The unwanted intimacy of the embrace brought Tegan's chin up. Resentment flamed ferociously within her, until almost immediately her resistance was overpowered by a wave of carnal yearning. Her mouth trembled in response to his long, slow survey.

Tegan was lost. Her lashes sank over dazzled, hazy eyes as she obeyed his unspoken command and melted against him, unaware of anything but the tumultuous need that coursed through her, the essential rightness of a surrender she didn't understand. So close together that they could have been one, they swayed to the music.

By turning her head slightly she could see her slender fingers, pale in the dim light, swallowed up by his darker ones. There was something almost barbaric in the juxtaposition of colours and shapes and textures, something wild and fierce in the sensations that rioted through her veins, setting fire to her emotions.

She was acutely aware of the muscles flexing in his thighs, the erotic heat of his shoulder beneath her fingers, the scent that taunted her nostrils. He smelt of virile male, of sun-heated plains and the violent, fascinating jungle, of a sharp, irresistible sexuality.

She was being, she thought dazedly, about as stupid as she could be. If she was going to salvage anything from this situation she had to maintain a business relationship with him. Yet here she was drifting around plastered against him as though the only thing on her mind was seduction.

He clouded the usual clarity of her thought processes with the taut sensuality, the aphrodisiac of his body. For of course that was all it was. Just a particularly potent form of attraction—exciting, but really nothing of importance.

You didn't get involved with clients, not emotionally. You had to learn to know them better than their own parents, but you didn't ever let it develop into anything else. Friendship itself was suspect; this blatant familiarity was infinitely more so. If she was stupid enough to fall prey to Kieran's particular brand of masculine virility she was going to be no use to Decorators Inc.

She had Blair, as well as Alana and the receptionist, to consider. The business was so finely balanced that they could only cope with the loss of the emir's palace if they held on to Raintree House. And if Blair didn't get back from El Amir Kieran would dispassionately, definitely throw them off the job. She didn't make the mistake of thinking that these moments spent in his arms meant he wouldn't do it. Somehow, Tegan thought, firming her mouth unconsciously, she had to persuade him not to deliver that final, crippling blow.

She began to ease back and this time he let her go. 'Goodness, it's hot,' she said, her normally clear voice muted and indistinct.

'Very. Humid, too, but that's Auckland.'

Although he spoke his usual tone she discerned mockery threading through the words. Well, she deserved it. She was behaving like a total twit.

At last the music stopped, and relief flooded through her, even though its ending brought a dour-faced Peter, and his pretty, flushed, very young partner, whom he introduced to Kieran with more speed than elegance, smiling through his teeth as the eighteen-year-old blushed and tried to act in a sophisticated manner. Just being with her made Tegan feel old and jaded.

Still, at the same age she'd been monumentally gauche, so who was she to be scornful because Fiona couldn't hide how she felt about the most attractive man in the room?

They talked commonplaces for the minute or so before the music resumed. Far too abruptly, so quickly that it was discourteous, Peter swept Tegan away, steering her immediately out through the doors and on to the almost deserted terrace. Over his shoulder she saw Kieran smile at Fiona Thompson, a genuine smile that made him seem younger, then say something. The girl's face lit up into incandescence. Still with the same smile he took her into his arms. So he had some gentleness in his personality after all; Tegan liked him for it.

'God,' Peter groaned, 'I thought I was doomed to dance with her all night. She's a dear little thing, but hell, she isn't you!' Stopping behind a sheltering oleander bush, he began to kiss Tegan expertly, his hands roaming, possessive, dragging her closer into his aroused body.

Tegan stiffened, and his hands became grasping, even a little cruel. With a quick jerk she wrenched herself free and stepped back, saying crisply, 'That's enough. I can't think of anything I've done that might give you the idea I'd enjoy that.'

'No?' he demanded, his flushed face petulant and aggrieved. 'Just the look of you is enough! If you didn't want to send out signals, why wear something like that outfit?'

'What should I have worn?' she asked, emphasising her words too sweetly. 'A sheet? A cloak that covers me from head to toe?'

'What's wrong with me?' he demanded belligerently, changing tack with the skill of a born negotiator. 'I saw you giving Kieran Sinclair long, meaningful looks while you were wrapped around him like a second skin—but of course he's a millionaire! If I were as rich as he is I'll bet you'd reconsider this ridiculous decision to stick to a platonic relationship.'

'No.' Tegan's voice was cool and crisp, all of the warmth leached away. 'I did tell you, right at the beginning, that I wasn't going to be anything more than a friend.'

'Hell, I didn't believe that. I still don't believe it.' He must have recognised the stony inflexibility of her expression for he took a deep breath and tried again. 'Tegan, you can't be that naïve! You must have known that I'd want a little more than that! Dry bread is all very well for a starving man, but not when there's wine and honey for the asking. What do you think I am, a eunuch?'

She said wearily, 'No, just a liar. Listen to me, Peter, because I'm not going to tell you again. I am not going to bed with you.'

His expression darkened. 'So you've been playing me for a fool! I'd heard you were a damned tease but I thought nobody who looked like you, all promises and laughter, could be frigid——'

'I think you'd better stop right there,' she said curtly. 'I'll get a taxi home.'

'You just do that, you lying bitch. You're notorious, did you know that?' The handsome face was twisted with a sudden, frightening rage. 'Cold as bloody charity, everyone told me. What are you saving it all for? If it's for your millionaire friend in there, you can forget it. He's a bloody cool customer, and he demands that his women front up with the goods. He's not going to be caught by someone who's got ice in her veins.'

Furious with him and with herself, Tegan turned on her heel and set off for the telephone.

She had just dialled the taxi company number when a large, masculine hand reached over and cut the connection.

Thinking it was Peter, she reacted with truculence. 'What do you——?'

'I'm going home now,' Kieran Sinclair said imperturbably. 'You can come with me.'

Her first impulse was to refuse. It was followed immediately by the sly insinuation that perhaps she could build on this tenuous interest of his and try to change his mind about Raintree House. She wasn't normally as defeatist as she had been that afternoon. Perhaps it was a hangover from that traumatic first meeting; had he made such an impression on her then that instead of responding with her usual determination she had just given up?

But she said, 'No, I came with Peter. It would look awful to go home with another man.'

Rodney Piper came bustling up, smiling, looking shrewdly from one to the other. 'On your way, you two?' he asked.

Kieran nodded. 'Like Ms Jones, I have to leave early. I'm trying to convince her to accept a lift with me, but she says that it would look bad as she came with young Hampshire.'

Something in his voice made Tegan look sharply at him. Did he guess—no, how could he know what had happened out there in the garden? He had been dancing with Fiona Thompson.

Rodney Piper said cheerfully, 'Nonsense, Tegan. Peter's staying until the end, so if you have to go home early he's not going to feel that you've walked out on him.'

But he would, because that was exactly what she would be doing.

'Take Kieran's offer of a lift,' the older man urged. It was clear that he was quite prepared to sacrifice her if he thought it would keep Kieran Sinclair happy. 'It's silly to take a taxi when he can drop you off on the way home.'

'I'll be out of his way. I live in Parnell.'

'It's not very far out of my way,' Kieran said calmly. Taking her assent for granted, he thanked his host for the evening, and with self-possessed skill got them out the door and into the street before she had the chance to object further.

The interior of his Jaguar had that smooth European feel of luxury—understated, yet powerful. A bit like the man, although the word understated didn't really fit him. If anything, Kieran Sinclair was larger than life in every respect.

'Your flat is in St Stephen's Avenue, isn't it?' he said, but not as though he needed directions.

'Yes. How did you know?'

'I had someone check on you.'

'You've got a nerve.' Her voice didn't convey the fury and outrage that raced through her, fuelled by the scene with Peter. It was difficult to keep it steady, almost thoughtful, but by exercising her not inconsiderable will-power she accomplished it. 'And what else did you find out?'

'That you were telling me the truth about your experience in the decorating business.'

He's given you the opening, her brain told her; take it, you fool! But she had to force herself to do it, nevertheless.

'Then if you know that,' she said, her voice flat with the effort it required, 'you also know that I'm more than capable of giving you a very comfortable, beautiful home.'

'Yes,' he said judicially. His cheek creased in a smile, ironic, very worldly. 'Your c.v. positively glows with praise. You have a great talent with older houses.'

'I'd like to finish Raintree House.'

'Did you do the scheme, and let your partner front it for you?'

She hesitated, then looked sideways. His spectacular good looks tended to overshadow the formidable severity of his features, she thought as her eyes measured the high forehead, the straight line of his nose and the

clear-cut mouth and jaw. His angular chin met the
world full-on. And it was so big; rarely was she dwarfed
by a man, but she certainly felt inconspicuous beside
Kieran Sinclair.

'Yes,' she said, throwing her cap over the windmill
with a vengeance. 'After our meeting ten years ago I
assumed that you wouldn't be at all interested in letting
me work for you.'

'You were right.' His voice was deep and cold, with a
note in it that hinted of strong emotions rigidly kept
under control by an iron will.

'But I know I can give you exactly what you want,'
she said, hating the hint of pleading in her voice. It went
against the grain to have to beg for this job, but if the
emir's palace was no longer viable then they were not
only strapped for work, but out of pocket, too. Blair
had spent a lot of time organising her scheme, and there
had been long-distance calls and plane trips in plenty.

'Can you?' He sounded amused, but when she went
to speak again he commanded, 'Leave it for now; I'm
going to think it over. What number in St Stephen's
Avenue?'

Blair's name had brought the memory of her plight
to mind. After giving him her number Tegan sat worrying about her partner, as well as her own far too vivid
reactions to the man beside her. She wanted to see her
lovely design through to fruition, and have the pleasure of bringing the house back to life. With any other
man 'thinking it over' might mean a change of mind,
but she shouldn't fool herself with wishful hopes.
Kieran Sinclair was hard all the way through.

In spite of her objections he came up to the door of
her apartment with her, but she didn't ask him in, and
he didn't suggest it, merely said, 'Goodnight,' with a

taunting inflexion when she had gone inside, and turned and walked away.

Tegan closed the door behind her with a sharp click and leaned back against it, a hand clenched over her heart. Her flat was cool and peacefully serene, and she loved it, but at the moment she could have been on the moon for all the comfort she got from it.

After several moments she went into the kitchen and drank a glass of cold water before checking her answerphone. When she saw the light blinking her heart sped up. Through crackle and static Blair's husky voice said hurriedly, 'Trust me to end up in a revolution! Don't worry, although the palace is a goner. We're leaving on a plane tomorrow morning, and I should be home in eighteen hours at the longest. See you then.'

'Oh, thank God,' Tegan whispered, setting the machine again. Relieved, she went to bed.

But on the radio the next morning the news was not so good. Overnight the bloodless coup had turned vicious. There were reports of sporadic small-arms fire throughout the capital city, the borders and the airfield had been closed and all communications were cut. No one had any idea what was happening to the twenty-three stranded New Zealanders.

Appalled, Tegan rang Gerald, and this time, thank heavens, he was at home.

'I don't know,' he said starkly when she asked what was happening. 'I've rung the Ministry of External Relations and Trade and they say they're trying to contact someone there, but there's absolutely nothing coming out of the place. I can only hope that Blair's still safe in the hotel.'

There was nothing helpful Tegan could say; they talked for a few more minutes, but she was profoundly uneasy. So, it was obvious, was Gerald.

After an hour of wandering aimlessly around her flat trying to stop her mind from conjuring up scenarios of escalating nastiness involving Blair, she decided that work was the only panacea. Once in the office she settled down at her desk, intent on fine-tuning the time chart she had prepared for Raintree House. This was the part she liked least—the nitty-gritty, the slog of organising. She began to make lists.

Some time later she put the pencil down and sat chewing her full bottom lip until a sudden glance at her watch sent her racing across the room to switch on the radio. The newsreader's solemn voice grated on her stretched nerves as she listened intently. There was still fighting in the capital of El Amir. Nothing had been heard of the expatriates trapped in the country, although at this moment fears were not held for their safety. A spokesman for the Ministry of External Relations and Trade said they were still trying to contact their council in the emirate.

Tegan's teeth bit into her lip. The only thing she could do for Blair was make sure she didn't lose Kieran's business.

Or was it? Last night he had said he had contacts in El Amir. Frowning deeply, she paced several times around the floor before, with an abrupt straightening of her shoulders, she went across to the filing cabinet and pulled out the one labelled 'Kieran Sinclair'. Quickly she dialled the telephone number.

She was bitterly regretting her temerity when he answered.

'It's Tegan Jones here,' she said, looking down at the white knuckles of her hand. 'You said you have contacts in El Amir—is there any chance of getting through to them?'

'Is Blair Cartwright still there?'

'Yes. Her husband's worried sick, and so am I.'

Quite gently, he said, 'If there's no way anyone else can get through, Tegan, I certainly can't.'

'No, I suppose not.' She hesitated, then said forlornly, 'Sorry I bothered you, I know it was stupid. It's just that I couldn't think of anything else to do.'

'She's almost certainly quite safe, merely suffering from boredom and the inconvenience of life without a few of the mod cons she's used to. This is an internal spat between factions in the country; it's got nothing to do with foreigners.'

'Spats have a habit of catching innocent bystanders in the crossfire.' Tegan drew a deep breath. 'Look, forget I rang. It's just a bad case of the jitters. Anyway, Blair's more than capable of looking after herself.'

After a short pause he said, 'Give me a couple of hours. I might be able to call in a few favours. Where are you?'

She gave him the telephone number and thanked him—thanks he brushed off casually.

Somewhat reassured, which was totally ridiculous because, however charismatic Kieran Sinclair was, there really wasn't anything he could do for Blair, she sat down once more at her desk. This time she managed to get some work done before he rang back an hour later.

'I haven't been able to get in touch with anybody in El Amir,' he said, 'but I have information from across the border, although I don't know how accurate it is. Rumour there has it that every foreigner in the city has been rounded up and taken into the mountains by troops from the rebellious faction.'

Tegan's blood ran cold. 'Why?'

'To keep them safe,' he said crisply. 'The coup plotters are well aware that it can do them no good to hurt any innocent foreigners, so they're taking them into their power base—the mountains—away from stray bullets and grenades. If it's true—and it seems the logical thing to do—Mrs Cartwright might well spend a few days roughing it, but she'll be safer than in a hotel with troops firing around her ears.'

'Yes.' Tegan swallowed. 'She'll even enjoy it, if I know Blair. I'll ring Gerald——'

'I don't want my name appearing in this,' he interrupted. 'I've already contacted the Ministry of External Relations and Trade, and they'll tell her husband.'

Just what sort of contacts did he have there? Tegan said quietly, 'I'm very grateful, and Blair will be, too, when she knows what you've done. Thank you.'

She could hear the dismissive shrug in his voice. 'It was nothing. Have you any spare time today?'

'Yes. I can give you a couple of hours now.'

'Then we'd better check out some furniture I have in store.'

Her heart skipped a beat. She asked slowly, 'Do I gather from that that you're prepared to let me do the job?'

'Yes.' His voice hardened. 'Mrs. Cartwright is out of the picture for at least a day or so, and I want to get into the house as soon as possible. When she gets back she can take over.'

'Yes, all right.' Arrogant swine, indeed! Alana had been quite correct in her assessment of the man.

'I'll pick you up in half an hour. We'll check out the furniture, and then we can go back to the house and you can tell me exactly what you plan to do.'

'If you give me the address of the storage warehouse I'll meet you there.' Her voice was toneless, the words clipped and sharp.

When she got there he was waiting outside, clad in superbly cut tan trousers and a camel-coloured shirt, his hair gleaming with gold highlights in the sun. As always, Tegan was astonished and affected by the sheer presence of the man, his size, and the surprising grace with which he moved. And by her own unruly reaction to all that casual, untrammelled masculinity.

Remember, she told her quickening body, he despises you.

CHAPTER THREE

THE furniture was not, as Tegan had half suspected it might be, unwieldy Victorian stuff. Instead, the wrappings revealed elegant and superbly cared for Georgian pieces, some of a quality that made her gasp. There was enough to fill Raintree House, as well as crates of china and silver and paintings.

'This is beautiful,' she said, trying to sound objective as she ran a caressing hand over a lyre-ended table, her fingers lingering on a patina so deep and mellow that it was like gazing into tawny port. 'Ideal! It will look stunning.'

'Yes.'

Kieran looked around the collection. Something in his expression, something bleak and controlled, puzzled Tegan. Did the pieces have bitter memories attached to them?

After a moment he said, 'Have you seen enough?'

'For the time being, anyway.'

'Right, let's go. You've got the list?'

She nodded. 'I'll follow you across.'

It was a magnificent day, warm and smooth and sweet, with a soft freshness in the air that melted on the tongue. But Tegan couldn't enjoy it. Tension held her an unwilling prisoner.

At the house she pulled in behind the silver and green Jaguar. Kieran stood with his back to her, looking at

what had once been a garden and was now a mass of
greenery struggling for survival beneath a shroud of
clutching vines. Frowning, Tegan eyed the incandescent violet flowers of a thousand convolvulus plants. It
was going to take time and hard work and loving care
to transform this garden into the showpiece it had been.

She switched off the engine and got out. Although
they were in the heart of suburbia the silence was thick,
almost tangible, except for the laughter of children and
the faint, staccato sound of a distant lawn-mower,
counterpointed by the shrill song of the cicadas.

'It's like Sleeping Beauty's castle,' she said. She had
to force herself to speak in a normal tone. 'I used to
drive past and wonder just what was in here.'

Kieran had swung around at her approach. Now he
smiled with more than a touch of irony. 'Before the
builders started it looked more like something from a
gothic novel.'

Tegan nodded. 'Somehow I always assumed that it
was Victorian,' she said, gazing up at the steep terra-
cotta-tiled roof and rendered walls, grey-green now with
mould and dirt, but showing how attractive the house,
with its leadlighted windows, must once have been. 'I
was really surprised when I saw it had been built in the
Twenties.'

Inserting a key into the lock, he said, 'The structure
is as solid as a rock, which is fortunate as there's been
no maintenance done for fifty years or so.'

Great things were happening inside. Tegan gazed
around with the fascinated interest she always felt when
she saw a house beginning to come to life again. The
whole house had been rewired, the plumbing replaced,
and the ceilings and walls insulated. The kitchen area
had been completely reconstructed, so that what was

once a warren of dark rooms was going to be light, open spaces, efficient and beautiful.

'I love that staircase.' Tegan's voice echoed across the wide, carpetless hall. Her eyes ran up the swooping, graceful curves of the structure. 'Imagine ripping down the original balustrade and replacing it with that narrow metal one! I wonder why they did it?'

'You have a craftsman who can replace it?'

'Yes, I know someone,' she said. 'There's an old man out at Titirangi who's a real artist with wood.'

Tegan's gaze followed Kieran's, noting the timber panelling of the dado, much in need of refinishing and polish and love, and the wide planks on the floor, dotted with ugly tacks around the edge where old carpet had been ripped up. 'The proportions are lovely,' she said softly, her eyes glowing with satisfaction. 'It's going to be the most beautiful house in Auckland when it's finished, I promise you.'

'I'm almost beginning to believe you,' he said drily. 'Let's go upstairs.'

As they went up the stairs his hand cupped her elbow. There was nothing remotely personal about his touch but the firm, confident grip summoned a sharp little tattoo of excitement. It was probably that which made Tegan stumble slightly. Instantly his fingers tightened, supporting her.

'Be careful,' he warned, waiting until she had regained her footing before setting off again. 'The stairs are safe, but those tacks look sharp. If you fall on one you could do yourself a nasty injury.'

'It was nothing to do with the stairs, just clumsiness.'

'I doubt whether you've ever made a clumsy move in your life.'

It should have been a compliment, but there was a note of cynicism in the deep voice that negated any such interpretation. Repressing the desire to look up and gauge exactly what he was thinking, she moved away as soon as they reached the top of the stairs, and made sure she didn't get so close again.

Upstairs were the bedrooms, a grim, antiquated bathroom, a huge linen cupboard big enough to sleep in, and a master suite. This storey had been in surprisingly good condition, so very little structural work was needed. However, there too the walls and ceilings had been insulated and stripped back to reveal the original plaster.

Tegan knew the measurements by heart, but she surveyed the rooms with half-closed eyes, mentally transferring the furniture into various positions.

In the master bedroom she said, 'Have you any ideas where you want things to go?'

He had indeed. Nodding, Tegan made quick notes, impressed by his excellent eye for proportion, and the decisiveness with which he spoke. So many of her clients were too afraid of their own inadequacy to make any suggestions at all.

When he had finished she looked around, smiling a little. It was always exciting to work on a house like this, to bring it back to its original beauty.

'What a superb view,' she murmured. 'It must be magical at night.'

Unlatching a window, she leaned out, straight into the canopy of a silkwood tree. Through the soft, rosy-pink tassel-flowers and feathery leaves the harbour sparkled blue as sapphires, shading further out into that magnificently blended hue on the borders of blue and green, the colour of Kieran Sinclair's eyes.

'Careful,' he warned lazily. 'Lean too far out and you'll end up in the tree.'

Swivelling her head, she surprised him surveying her legs with a speculative, narrow-eyed gaze. Something jolted inside her, a fundamental shift and play of emotion that wreaked havoc with her equilibrium. The knuckles of her hands whitened as she pushed herself back inside.

Closing the window with a sharp slam, she asked huskily, 'How about downstairs? What furniture do you want where?'

He smiled. 'We'll go and take a look.'

Downstairs the rotting horror of a kitchen and the puzzle of pantries and sculleries and large cupboards— or tiny rooms—had been ripped out to make room for a new kitchen and a casual sitting- and dining-room. Further along, more or less intact, was an exquisitely proportioned formal drawing-room with patterned plaster cornices and ceiling mouldings in remarkably good condition, and a huge dining-room panelled in kauri.

Next door was another panelled room lined by bookcases. Presumably the last of the Raintrees had spent most of her time in there, as it showed signs of heavier wear than any of the other rooms.

'The cabinet-maker will check out all the panelling and woodwork,' Tegan said, smoothing over a place where someone had hammered in a nail then pulled it out again, leaving a jagged tear in the lovely wood. Such vandalism hurt something inside her. 'Tell me how you see this room.'

'It will be my office at home, so there'll be a computer and a filing cabinet, as well as a desk, but it will also be a sitting-room and library. I want it to be comfortable and efficient, with a sofa before the fire and chairs. And I want it finished first.'

'Television set?'

He hesitated, then nodded. 'A small one, and an audio system, but not where they will be obvious. There's a red Persian rug that would go well in here.'

Tegan made swift sketches and notes. 'It would help if I know how you live, what things are important to you in a house, what things you hate. Just very quickly and broadly.'

His wide shoulders moved in a shrug. 'I get up and go to work like any other man. When I come home I usually swim for some time before settling down to dinner. I read a lot, which is why I want this room to be comfortable. I go out quite frequently. I don't do any business entertaining at home, although I want the house to be able to cope with the occasional big party as well as less formal evenings. I enjoy talking. I hate anything cheap and fashionable and meretricious. I collect architectural prints of New Zealand buildings.'

'Sounds an idyllic life,' she said non-committally, scribbling. 'I'll need you to let the storage warehouse know that I'm entitled to go and look through your stuff.'

There was a moment's taut silence. Finally, he said with a palpable reluctance, 'I suppose so. Very well, I'll do that.'

Did he think she was going to steal his treasure? Tegan pushed the odd little hurt to one side. Eventually he would learn that he could trust her.

'When you've finished here,' he said curtly, 'I want you to take a look at what used to be the servant's quarters. They're to be turned into a flat for a housekeeper. I'll meet you there in, say, twenty minutes?'

'Yes, that should see me through here.'

She didn't watch him go, bending her head over her sketchpad as she forced her mind back to the work in hand.

Twenty minutes later she picked her way to the other end of the house, past the shambles of the kitchen and its satellites to the three rooms which had once been the servants' quarters.

Kieran was standing in the biggest one, his brows drawn together in a frown, looking around as though the place offended him. 'You'll need to consult my housekeeper about this,' he said calmly. 'I'll set up a meeting here on Monday.' He directed a level, unsmiling look at her. 'She is to get exactly what she wants, even if it is contrary to the latest dogma of the decorators' bible,' he said with curt clarity.

Tegan pushed a strand of thick black hair away from her cheek. 'I design rooms to suit the people who are going to be living in them,' she returned just as brusquely.

He watched her with half-closed eyes before smiling with a cynicism that set her teeth on edge. 'Have I offended your professional pride? Sorry.'

He wasn't, of course, but she inclined her head in what she hoped he'd take as acceptance of his apology.

'Did the architect show you the room under the kitchen? He wants to turn it into a games-room.'

'It would be perfect for that,' she said evenly.

He lifted his brows. 'No further ideas?'

'Ideas,' she said, irritated by his assumption that she forced designs and opinions on to her clients, 'are my stock-in-trade.'

His brows lifted. 'I thought your very attractive body was that,' he returned smoothly.

Unable for a moment to believe what she'd heard, Tegan stared at him. Sheer shock kept her dumb for several seconds, but even as she opened her mouth to storm at him she thought of Blair, probably alone and afraid in El Amir, pinning her hopes on this job. Was he looking for an excuse to get rid of her? He wouldn't think twice about terminating the contract. Hell, he had enough money to fight them through every court in the land; he might not win, but he would make their victory a Pyrrhic one.

Stonily, she said, 'Ten years ago my body, if I recollect correctly, was two yards of no particular appeal. I suppose I should be grateful you've changed your mind in the interim. However, I'm not. I didn't then and I don't now use my body to get me jobs, if that's what you were implying. Shall we go and look at this room?'

'You appear to have total recall of what I said then.'

She bared her teeth at him. 'If I were at all inclined to drama I might say they were seared into my brain. I've never been called a whore since then.'

'I don't remember saying that.'

'You did.'

'Then I'm sorry,' he said, astounding her. 'It was a cruel thing to say to a girl as young as you were, whatever you had done.'

He turned, leading the way down a flight of stairs with an expression on his features that could only be called remote, Tegan decided savagely. His unexpected apology both astonished and enraged her; clearly he hadn't changed his mind about her—he just thought he'd been harsh on a young girl. Rather proud that she hadn't hit him across his handsome face, she followed him.

As the house was built on the side of the hill the room had full-length windows on three sides, and a back wall that butted into the slope.

Calling on her professionalism, Tegan said, 'It could be a games-room. It's more than big enough to take a billiard table, and the stairs mean you wouldn't have to go outside to get to it. Do you play billiards?'

'Occasionally,' he said drily. 'If forced to. I'd rather it was a casual sitting-room. The swimming-pool is just through that thicket of eleagnus and convolvulus.'

Tegan looked around. 'Yes, it could be lovely, especially for children. It would make a perfect pool-room and playroom. And the little rooms at the back could be easily turned into a dressing-room and shower.' She frowned, visualising the plan. 'They're under the kitchen, so it shouldn't be too difficult to hook up plumbing. Isn't there a tap in there already? I'm pretty sure I saw one yesterday.'

'I don't know,' he said, turning away. 'I'll go and check. Don't come with me; the cleaners missed those two rooms so they're seething with spiders.'

Tegan sighed. 'I don't mind spiders much. Besides, we've already been introduced.'

The rooms were small and dank and cold, and in the wan light of the naked light bulbs the spiderwebs assumed an almost cosmic significance. Yet Tegan ignored them and their inhabitants. Her whole attention was fixed on the man who stood beside her. A strange mixture, she thought, ruthless yet with a few streaks of compassion in him. And trying to work out why she should be so interested in him in spite of her antagonism was only going to intensify her feelings. Better by far to ignore the fact. She peered through the dimness, searching for the tap.

'Yes, there it is,' she said briskly. 'So there must be some plumbing down here, although heaven knows what state it will be in.'

'I imagine the architect will know. Seen enough?'

Tegan nodded. Back in the big room, unnerved by the size of the spiders lurking in the arras of webs, she twisted, checking herself apprehensively.

A long-fingered hand on her shoulder turned her around so that he could see her back. 'All clear,' he said. 'No hitch-hikers.'

But he didn't release her. Like an animal surprised in the open, Tegan stood very still, looking up into a face that was suddenly sharply angular, the golden skin drawn tight over the autocratic framework. His lashes drooped, but beneath them she could see a narrow line of colour, blazing, translucent. Her heart lurched. Sunlight poured in through the windows, picking out the clean, strong lines of his face, setting shadows on his cheeks from incredibly long, thick, straight lashes, detailing with loving precision the hard, sculpted line of his mouth.

'I'm sorry,' he said softly. 'I didn't realise spiders frightened you.'

He knew damned well that it wasn't the spiders that robbed her skin of its small amount of colour, turning her sallow. That knowledge was written in his smile, in the limpid, mocking gleam in his eyes.

'I'm all right,' Tegan said huskily, taking a small, involuntary step backwards. He released her instantly, but she was left with a feeling of great danger narrowly averted, of a precipice almost opening at her feet.

Quickly, the words almost tripping over each other, she asked, 'Why did you buy this house? There are plenty of places you could have chosen that won't take nearly as much money or effort or time to turn into the place you want.'

'I like old houses. I grew up in a house very like this in Christchurch. I like room to breathe, and I like privacy. Raintree House offers me all of those.' He looked at her quizzically. 'I also like to put my mark on anything I do, and the apartment I live in now, although very modern and comfortable, has about as much soul as a fillet of fish.'

Tegan's rich laughter made him smile. 'I'll bet if they heard your opinion of their work the architect and decorators who organised your apartment's décor would cut their throats—or possibly yours. But if I remember, in your original brief to us you said that you liked modern rooms.'

He opened the door and stood back as she went out into the hot, bright day. A few paces along was the silkwood tree that made a canopy outside the main suite. Without discussion they stopped in its feather shade.

Kieran leaned against the smooth bole, hands in his pockets, his face impassive apart from the shimmering amusement in his eyes. 'I do. I don't like rooms restored so faithfully to the original that all freedom is stifled. Ms Richmond's scheme actually was quite good, as far as it went. I turned her down because instead of listening to what I wanted she prepared the scheme she would have liked if she owned Raintree House. As for the architect and decorator, they'd probably call me a philistine.'

'And would they be right?' Tegan asked demurely.

He laughed, head thrown back. Several investigating rays of the sun through the fragile leaves lit his hair to a glory of tawny fire. Lost in the first real laugh Tegan had heard from him, he seemed young and almost innocent, without the pulsing undercurrent of danger that once attracted and repelled her. But almost immediately experience and worldliness took over once more, banishing the fleeting glimpse of the boy who had been Kieran Sinclair long ago before the world had stained his soul.

'No,' he said blandly. 'And, although you possibly consider it heresy, I don't give a damn what they think.'

No, of course he wouldn't. He probably didn't give a damn what anyone thought of him. How wonderful to have that arrogant, bone-deep confidence. Wonderful for him, anyway—highly intimidating to everyone else!

'This garden must have been lovely once.' Tegan spoke hurriedly, more shaken than she was prepared to admit.

'It will be lovely again. The landscaper and his gang are sharpening their tools prior to satisfying their souls with an orgy of pruning and clearing and manuring. When the grounds are clear and I can see what I've got, he'll decide how and where to fit in a few other things I want.'

His hand closed, warm and sure and strong, about her arm. It was like a claim, a bold statement of ownership, and it brought all Tegan's fears pelting back. When she looked up at him she was ensnared by the ruthless brilliance of his gaze.

'Time to go.' Kieran's voice was steady. 'Be careful as you walk along here—the ground is uneven.'

Back home Tegan worked some time on ideas for the playroom, free-associating, then laid down her pen with a sigh and stood up. Dizziness made her head spin.

'Lunch,' she muttered after a quick glance at her watch. It was after two o'clock, and she needed food at regular intervals, otherwise her system rebelled.

She had forgotten to check the answerphone, but she saw now that a little red light was blinking impatiently at her. 'All right,' she told it, hiding a clutch of fear with brisk bossiness.

Gerald had left her a message. 'I've just got word,' his voice said agitatedly, 'that Blair's been taken up into the mountains. My contact at the Ministry says it's for her protection, but he sounded damned cagey to me. Ring me when you get back, will you, Tegan?'

Taking time only to make and eat a cheese and to-mato sandwich, she went straight around to the Cartwrights' flat and spent an hour with him, trying to give him some sort of comfort. She didn't succeed; he was convinced this latest development was sinister. Tegan wished she could tell him what Kieran had said, but kept her word.

Anyway, she thought when at last she arrived back home, it would sound much better coming from Kieran. He came over as absolutely trustworthy, the sort of man who knew what he was talking about. He'd make a good politician—all that star quality, and dependable to boot. But it was quite impossible to imagine him in such a position. He had too much autonomy to be a good party man.

Ruthlessly dragging her mind away from him, she drove across town and played tennis with a friend, then stayed to dinner.

No further word came through about Blair during the rest of the weekend. All communications with El Amir were still blocked, and according to the news the fighting had escalated. Clearly the rebels had known what they were doing when they whisked their hostages away into the mountains.

On Monday morning Tegan discussed the situation with a shocked Alana, then settled down to check her mail. A moment later the telephone buzzed. A crisp, cultivated female voice identified itself as Kieran Sinclair's secretary, and informed her that Mr Sinclair's housekeeper would meet her at Raintree House at ten o'clock.

'Hang on, I'll just check ... Yes, I can make that,' Tegan said, also crisply. 'Thank you.'

She put the receiver down with a definite click. The nerve of them! Expecting her to jump when they cracked the whip.

The housekeeper, Mrs Webber, was not at all what Tegan had expected. A tall, raw-boned woman of about forty-five, she had hair dyed black, a definite English accent and just as definite ideas of what she wanted in her flat—ideas Tegan scribbled down as they walked through the rooms.

'That's fine,' she said when they'd finished. 'I'll get some swatches ready, and bring them to you.'

'I'll meet you here,' Mrs Webber to her. 'I'll find it easier to decide if I can see them where they're going to be used. I won't have to make up my mind straight away, will I?' It was the first sign of uncertainty she had displayed.

'Goodness, no; keep the swatches for as long as you need them. Play around with them, see them in all the lights, make sure they look good at night.'

'That's all right, then. Oh, and Miss Sinclair told me to tell you that she'll need to see you too, as one of the bedrooms is going to be for her.'

Tegan said firmly, 'I'll contact her myself, then, and make an appointment that's convenient for both of us.' And immediately felt mean, as the morning's display of arrogance hadn't been the housekeeper's fault.

Mrs Webber knew what she was getting at, however. Shrewd brown eyes twinkled suddenly. 'They don't actually *mean* to be so high-handed,' she said, adding with a lurking smile, 'Just be thankful that it's not the old man, Kieran's father, you're dealing with. I never met him myself, but from all accounts he was uppity enough to make a saint weep.'

Not content with being arrogant himself, he'd passed it on to his son, and possibly his daughter. Tegan gave a vague smile. 'Unfortunately I'm no saint—I'm more likely to swear than cry.' Which was not quite true. They needed this job so much that she had to keep a very tight rein on her temper. 'Well, that's all we need to do. Would you like to have a look through the rest of the house and see where they've got to?'

'No, I can't. I have to be back home in quarter of an hour. Thank you, Miss Jones.'

Surely Kieran didn't expect such rigid time-keeping? Tegan watched the trim, upright figure of the housekeeper fold into a small car, then went back inside. She had to consult the builder about one or two things.

Two weeks passed slowly. The situation in El Amir was forgotten by the news media, and all of Gerald's importuning couldn't coax any more information from the Ministry.

On Thursday Tegan went to Raintree House with the swatches for Mrs Webber, leaving her to look at them while she conferred with the painter in the drawing-room. She was on her way back when Kieran and another man walked in through the front door. In this persona, wearing clothes imbued with a muted air of affluence that spoke of old money and plenty of it, Kieran Sinclair was completely overwhelming.

A frown drew his dark brows together, but he said without any audible expression, 'Yes, of course. Mrs Webber's choosing her colours today.'

Tegan smiled at the man with him. 'Well, she's looking at the swatches.'

'She might perhaps need your professional help?'

And damn you, too. Tegan directed a warm, tantalising smile his way. Pleased to see a flash of fire in the sea-green depths of his eyes, she told him, 'She made it more than clear that she didn't want anyone fussing around her while she made up her mind. But she has probably had enough time to decide which ones she likes. I'm on my way to see.' She nodded to the man beside Kieran, aware that he had been watching her with an interest that wasn't in the least tepid.

'No,' he said immediately, 'surely she must need to spend more time on such an important decision. Kieran, introduce us, please.'

Kieran's expression hardened, but he said, 'Of course,' and introduced them.

The newcomer was Rick Hannibal, who worked for Kieran; he gave Tegan a charming, very pleasant smile, which made her like him instantly. He didn't have a quarter of Kieran's charisma, but she was prepared to bet her grandmother's garnet and seed-pearl bracelet that he was a much nicer person.

'You didn't tell me your interior decorator is a stunning beauty,' he said to Kieran, smiling broadly. 'You've been holding out on us.'

Kieran's brows lifted, giving his expression a sudden satirical quality. 'It didn't exactly come up, as I recall,' he said shortly. 'Anyway, now you've met her, let's get going. We've no time to waste.'

After directing an amused glance at Tegan, Rick Hannibal obediently went off with him, saying something in which the words *possessive* and *jealous* were emphasised so that they were loud enough for Tegan to hear. Clearly he was on terms of intimacy with his boss. Not your normal corporate underling.

He was also wrong. 'Little do you know, chum,' Tegan said beneath her breath as she turned away. 'He's very aware of me, just as I am of him, but he wouldn't touch me if I were the last woman on earth!'

Mrs Webber had made her decisions. In each room there remained only one swatch each of paint and carpet and fabric.

'That was quick!' Tegan exclaimed. 'I thought you wanted lots of time to decide. Are you sure you wouldn't like to keep them so you can see what they look like at night?'

The older woman smiled a little sheepishly. 'No, I took them into one of those downstairs rooms and turned on the light, so I know what they look like in artificial light. I just didn't want to be rushed. I can make up my mind all right when nobody's pushing me, but I get a bit dithery when someone's saying, "Hurry up, hurry up, make up your mind now!" Those ones are the ones I like. Pretty autumn colours—they've always been my favourites.'

'Well, I wish all my clients made up their minds as quickly as you,' Tegan told her cheerfully, beginning to stack the rejects into a bag.

'It helps when you don't have to pay for it,' Mrs Webber said, smiling ironically. 'Now, is there anything else you want me for?'

'No, for the time being that's fine. As soon as the
rooms are ready I'll get the curtains hung. Had you
thought of a bedspread and upholstery?'

Mrs Webber nodded reluctantly. 'Mr Sinclair said I
was to get what I wanted,' she said after a moment, 'but
I don't want to be spending a great lot of money on
them.'

Of course it paid to be good to the hired help, but
even so... Tegan's respect for Kieran went up a few
notches. 'Would you like me to look at your furniture
and——?'

Mrs Webber said resolutely, 'No, I think I'll just wait
until we get into the house, and then we'll have a better
idea of how they look in my rooms. Thank you, Miss
Jones. Is Mr Sinclair here?'

'Yes, with a Rick Hannibal.' The memory of that
shared smile brought a soft curve to Tegan's lips.

'Mr Hannibal is Miss Andrea's friend.' Mrs Webber's
voice was very level, her gaze direct and a little hard.
Clearly she was protective of Kieran's beautiful sister.
After a moment she finished, 'I'd better be on my way,
then. Goodbye.'

Tegan labelled the rest of the swatches, sat cross-
legged on the floor to make notes, then wandered out
to the car, heaving the swatches and her briefcase on to
the back seat. As she closed the car door she wondered
why, if Rick Hannibal was Andrea's friend, she had
been snuggling so intimately up to another man at the
Pipers' party? No wonder Kieran had stiffened when
he'd seen them together.

Peter's voice echoed unpleasantly in her inner mind.
I didn't know they had a cure for nymphomania, he had
said, or something like it. Was Andrea promiscuous? If
that was the case, poor Rick. And poor Andrea.

Just as she turned the key in the ignition Kieran walked out of the front door and beckoned imperatively. Leaving the engine on, she wound down the window and waited.

'I want to see you,' he said brusquely. 'I'll send a car for you and we'll go out to lunch today.' He forestalled her equally abrupt refusal. 'There's news from El Amir.'

'All right, then,' Tegan said slowly. 'But you don't need to send a car; I can drive myself.'

'I have an appointment I can't get out of, one that should be finished by twelve o'clock, but might not, so it'll be easier if you use the car. Then you won't have to wait in the restaurant.' Rick Hannibal came up to stand beside him, his open, handsome face alight with unconcealed interest. Kieran finished, 'So be ready from twelve-thirty on.'

Who did he think she was? Employing her did not give him the right to order her around like that. Squashing the desire to tell him to go to hell, Tegan nodded, her expression cold and aloof. She would do far more than go to lunch with a dangerous man if it meant finding out more about Blair's situation.

He stood back. 'See you later.'

'Yes. Goodbye, Mr Hannibal.'

'Rick,' he said cheerfully. 'I'm looking forward to seeing more of you, Tegan.'

Tegan put the car into gear and drove off. Just once her eyes flicked to the rear-view mirror, to catch the two men's faces, Kieran's dark and chiselled as he spoke rapidly, his companion's for once without the conspiratorial smile.

Her pulses were still humming but she managed to get that instinctive spark of response under control. After all, she couldn't help the way her body went wild when

she saw Kieran Sinclair; what she could do, and had to
do, was make sure that the crazy physical reaction didn't
seduce her into behaving stupidly.

By the time the long, navy blue chauffeur-driven car
arrived outside the showroom of Decorators Inc, Tegan
had donned the clothes she kept at the office for just
such an emergency. After carefully re-applying lipstick
she smoothed her sunflower-print skirt, glad that she
had spent such a horrendous amount of money on a
soft, unlined checked jacket in matching pale rust and
gold checks to tone down the exuberance of the skirt.
But it was a militant gleam that lit her eyes to pure,
glittering gold jewels as she settled into the back seat.

Kieran Sinclair would soon learn that he wasn't going to be able to move her around like a chess piece
whenever he felt like it. Organising the decorating of his
house did not give him unlimited access to her time.

The car smelt of leather and money. Obviously,
owning a merchant bank was profitable. Of course, that
intangible aura of authority and status would give him
away even without perks like the car. Kieran Sinclair
was at the top of his chosen career; no doubt he had
trampled mercilessly over anyone who got in his way.

How on earth had he come to own a bank at his age?
True, it had been a family one, but, even so, to oust a
couple of uncles must have entailed the use of a considerable amount of ruthlessness. In Tegan's experience,
men didn't give up power easily. Usually it had to be
wrested from them.

But Kieran's air of *importance*, for lack of a better
word, was inborn, not merely the result of reaching the
top in his career. Closing her eyes for a moment, Tegan
tried to imagine him in his underwear; according to
Blair, this was a sure-fire way of cutting anyone down

to size. It had always worked before. But Tegan had given her mind licence, and it took it.

Images danced behind her closed lids, so that she shifted uncomfortably, trying to relax muscles that were suddenly tense. Kieran, golden in near-nudity, all coiled, masculine strength with an effortless potency that promised physical rapture...

You only had to look at him, she thought with a muffled groan, to know that he would be a wonderful lover. What was it, that mysterious aura that marked the favoured numbers of both sexes, the glow of sexuality promising forbidden, erotic delights? It had innumerable names, but no one had ever been able to pin down what exactly it was.

And neither could she, beyond accepting that Kieran possessed it in abundance, and that she was finding it difficult to resist. That moment of unguarded imagination had revealed one thing; shorn of everything else, clad only in briefs, Kieran Sinclair had still very definitely been someone.

But she was not going to show even the remotest interest in him. She was going to be cool and businesslike and self-possessed. *Totally* professional.

Seabreeze was a restaurant built on one of the old ferry wharves after increasing private car ownership and the Harbour Bridge had denied the ferries their commuters. A starkly modern building with a magnificent view over the harbour, it specialised in superb seafoods, superbly cooked. It was very fashionable and inordinately expensive. Tegan had been there only once before.

After giving her name to the receptionist and being divested of her jacket, she was handed on to a very dignified head waiter who escorted her across the polished floor to a table in the window where Kieran Sinclair was getting to his feet. In these sophisticated surroundings he looked as impressive, as uncompromisingly masculine as he had at the house.

His smile was a masterpiece, registering approval of her appearance, mockery, and a complete understanding of her inner anger. Too late Tegan realised she should have insisted on retaining her jacket—its classic lines at least made her look businesslike. Now, reduced to a rust silk shirt and the sunflower skirt, she was deprived of armour. Even her long gold earrings, she thought ruefully as she slid into her chair, although they suited her, were obviously fake, and definitely had nothing to do with power-dressing.

'You have great style,' Kieran said.

Tegan's lashes flew up. Was he a mind-reader? No, that was certainly a gleam of appreciation in the cool, aquamarine depths of his eyes.

'Thank you,' she murmured, as though people told her this every day of her life. 'So have you.'

This did surprise him. His mouth quirked, then he laughed. 'Thank *you*. Do you want to order now, or have a drink first?'

'Order, now, please; I have a client in——' she consulted the large businesslike watch on her slim wrist '—an hour.' There, that should put him in his place.

'What would you like?' He merely looked towards the waiter but the man came hurrying towards them as though summoned by bells.

'Oh—scallops and salad, thank you.'

'I'll have the same,' he told the waiter. Just as miraculously as the first one, the wine waiter appeared, presenting the list. Kieran cast an eye down it. 'A half-bottle of Reserve Chardonnay, thank you.'

Tegan waited until both waiters had gone before saying carefully, 'This is delightful, of course, but you could have made an appointment to see me during working hours, like everyone else.'

'I'm busy during working hours,' he informed her in an entirely reasonable tone. He said nothing more, but sat watching her with an oblique smile curving the corners of his mouth.

'That's what appointments,' she replied far too sweetly, 'are for.'

'Don't you like giving up your lunch-hour to business? I'd always assumed that decorators did a lot of hustling after hours.'

He had her there, of course. Her unruly tongue had run away with her, and it didn't pay to give this man any opening at all. But—*hustling*?

'As in your business,' she said, the sweetness in her tone assuming saccharine proportions, 'contacts are important, of course, but at the end there's nothing like a good job well done to bring in the customers.'

'Then let's just hope that you can interpret your ideas well enough to make visitors to Raintree House swoon with pleasure.'

Tegan surveyed him through narrowed eyes, but he met her fulminating glare with such bland insouciance that in spite of her caution her compressed mouth relaxed into an unwilling smile.

'That's better,' he said, not attempting to hide his amusement. 'I was sure you had to have a sense of humour among all that Celtic fire.'

She was taken aback. 'Celtic fire? That's a new term for it. My teachers used to say I had no control over my temper and my father says I'm far too quick off the mark. In future I'll tell him it's Celtic fire, inherited from him.'

'Like the long Celtic bones, and that ivory skin? What does your father do?'

Tegan had managed to drag her fascinated eyes away from the austere angles and planes of his face, transferring her gaze to the magnificent panorama of harbour and islands and small volcanic cones that made Auckland so different from any other city; but at this her head swivelled.

'He's a doctor,' she answered warily. 'On the Coromandel peninsula.'

He nodded. At that moment the waiter arrived. When everything had been set before them, the wine tasted and approved, and the waiter gone, Kieran continued, 'A magical place to grow up in.'

'I loved it,' she said, adding, 'But it can be a prison, too.'

'Yes, I imagine it can.' He was watching her too closely for her composure to remain steady.

She said stiffly, 'You told me that you had something to tell me about Blair.'

He lifted his brows. 'Eat up,' he ordered. And waited until, mutinously, she picked up her knife and fork, before continuing, 'I don't think I actually said that— if I gave you that impression, I'm sorry, because I know very little. However, my contacts have heard a whisper that the rebel government are not going to hand their guests back too quickly. Their value as hostages against their government's behaviour has been recognised.'

CHAPTER FOUR

COLD dismay lurched into her stomach. Numbly she put down her fork and knife, but Kieran commanded, 'Eat up. Starving yourself is not going to help anyone.'

Without tasting a thing, Tegan chewed mechanically at the soft cream and apricot shellfish. 'I know,' she said with a twisted smile. 'She's probably having the time of her life—she does that, makes the best of any situation she finds herself in. I just wish I *knew* she was all right.'

'For what it's worth, I imagine they're being treated as honoured guests.'

'Poor Gerald,' Tegan said, putting down her fork again.

'That's the husband?'

'Yes. He's desperate, but he doesn't seem to be able to get anything out of the Ministry people. They keep stalling him.'

'Ineffectual, is he?'

Of course he'd think so; in a similar situation no doubt Kieran would have the Ministry people totally intimidated, singing their hearts out to him. Money and power talked in ruthless accents. Tegan looked at him with dislike.

'Gerald's very nice. He's sensitive, and kind and thoughtful——'

'He sounds like a wimp. Is that the sort of man you like—one who'll let you run all over him?'

Would any man who didn't match up to Kieran's strength be treated with that fine, tolerant scorn? Tegan shook her head. 'There's a difference between being weak and being compassionate. Gerald's a darling, and he's almost frantic with worry. Can I tell him what you said?'

'I suppose so, but don't give him any sources.'

'What are your contacts there?'

'Bandits,' he said. 'I spent a season with them once.'

Dying to know all about it, but not confident enough to ask, Tegan stared at him. His dark face cracked into a grin that made him suddenly much younger, infinitely more reckless than the calculating, collected banker she had come to know. 'I'll tell you about it one day, when we've got an hour or two to waste,' he said.

Then he looked past her. Something ugly flickered in his eyes. It was gone immediately; he rose with his customary courtesy and there was certainly no hint of antagonism in the smile he gave the beautiful woman who stopped beside their table.

'Hello, Kieran.' Andrea Sinclair reached up to kiss his cheek, her mouth curved in a guarded smile.

'I didn't know you were eating here today,' he said, completely unruffled. And to Tegan, 'My sister, Andrea. Andrea, this is Tegan Jones.'

Andrea extended a hand; the smile diminished appreciably. 'Ah, the decorator,' she purred. 'I saw you at the Pipers' dreary little do, didn't I? How nice to meet you,' speaking in a tone that made a lie of the words.

Tegan shook hands with something like distaste. She had taken one of those instantaneous dislikes, and it hurt that it should be to Kieran's sister. Aloud she replied, 'How do you do, Miss Sinclair?'

'So formal!' Amusement deepened in the large, carefully made-up eyes. Andrea Sinclair looked limpidly from Tegan's still face to her brother's arrogant one. 'Call me Andrea; everyone always does. I don't get the sort of respect Kieran commands. I want to talk to you about my room, Miss Jones.' More of that not too subtle mockery as her voice lingered over Tegan's surname.

Tegan looked at Kieran. The hard, handsome face was expressionless. He said indifferently, 'You can discuss that any time.'

'Oh, lovely. What fun I'm going to have!' She sent a sly, sideways glance at her brother. 'I do tend to have ideas that are a little over-the-top, but I dare say Kieran will put a budget limit on me, so we'll have to do the best we can within that. Make an appointment some time, Miss Jones. I'll see you later, Kieran.' She kissed his cheek again and was gone to join a man—not Rick Hannibal—across the room.

Designer clothes, Tegan thought. You could always tell. Andrea Sinclair looked superb. No wonder Rick Hannibal was smitten. However, for all her stunning beauty, Kieran's sister had a driven, almost febrile air, and, judging by her choice of companions, she was nowhere near as smitten as Rick was.

Her arrival certainly had a strong effect on her brother. Kieran had retreated to the inbound fastness of his courtesy; sneaking a glance at his face, Tegan shivered.

'Would you like to see *River Run Deep* tonight?' he asked abruptly.

She hesitated. The play, a thoughtful, provocative drama set in Otago, was a critical success, and tickets were almost impossible to get.

She should say, 'Not likely,' and mean it. Instinct told her, common sense warned her, her sense of self-preservation positively shouted at her that she should say no very firmly, and spent the rest of her life being thankful she had had the guts to do it.

Kieran Sinclair was dangerous.

It was madness—recklessness of the worst sort—to even consider——

'I didn't know you were a coward,' he said, his voice cool and subtly taunting.

Subduing a reflexive wariness, she fixed him with a long, direct stare. 'I detest people who try to manipulate me,' she said at last, her voice level and hard.

His smile was a masterpiece of irony. 'One of the things I like about you is your intelligence.'

What are the others? For a horrified moment she thought she had said the words aloud, but of course she hadn't. However, he laid his utensils down and picked up her slender hand, his tanned fingers so startling a contrast to the matt texture of her skin that she almost winced. His thumb moved gently over her palm, setting off fires beneath its inexorable path, until it came to rest over the blue veins in her wrist.

'And that,' he said softly, 'is another thing I find very interesting.'

Tegan's head was bent but she could feel the brilliant stiletto of his gaze boring into her. 'What do you want?' she asked through stiff lips, a question torn from the inner reaches of her heart.

'I don't know,' he said slowly, as though she had surprised him.

Surprised herself, she lifted her face to discover him looking at her with something like astonishment, perhaps even a hint of resentment.

Obviously choosing his words carefully, he said, 'I haven't been able to get you out of my mind. I'm not usually a gambler, but—occasionally I like to take a chance on something. You do too, I think.'

Tegan had spent the last ten years of her life stringently avoiding any emotional risk. How had he discerned that hidden, repressed tendency to recklessness? The temptation to surrender to it, to follow and see where it led her, was almost irresistible. Since the episode with Sam she had led a life of unnatural caution; was it time for her to allow this wild yearning for the forbidden some freedom?

'Yes,' Kieran said, as though answering her unspoken question. 'Shall we start again, Tegan?'

His voice was deep, many-layered, and intensely, seductively persuasive—the voice of the tempter, but there was a note in it which told her he wanted this as much as she did.

But she had to get something straight. 'What about Sam?' she asked quietly. 'You called me names...'

His mouth twisted. 'I thought you were a hard little piece, out for what you could get.'

Watching him with wide, angry eyes, she shook her head.

'So I realise now,' he said, shrugging. 'I don't suppose you understood what you were doing to him. Forget about Sam—and forget, if you can, that I lost my temper and called you names I don't suppose you'd ever heard before.'

'I—all right,' she said, the words escaping her startled lips before she had time to call them back.

For a second longer his thumb rested on her pulse, then he folded her fingers over her palm in an oddly tender little gesture and gave her hand back to her. Now that it was too late her innate prudence was shrieking at her. What on earth had possessed her to agree—and what on earth had she agreed to?

But even as she began to formulate the question he said calmly, 'Then I'll pick you up at seven-fifteen. How about supper afterwards?'

'Yes. I'd like that.' She knew she sounded mechanical, but for the life of her she couldn't infuse any expression into her voice. Even the skin on her face felt stiff.

He glanced around the room, a cynical smile tugging at the corners of his mouth. 'We seem to be attracting some attention. Why don't you pretend that this is merely a business lunch, and tell me how far you've got with organising the house?'

Embarrassed, Tegan collected enough composure to present several points for discussion in a more or less coherent manner, taking notes as he told her exactly what he wanted done, until coffee was set before him. A quick glance at her watch revealed she had time for one cup. She certainly needed something to cut the alcohol; it didn't seem possible that one glass of wine could make her brain buzz and excitement expand inside her, as tangible as indigestion and not much more pleasant, but it was happening.

Tegan had the stupid feeling that she had handed her life over to Kieran, that from now on she could cease to be her own person and belong to him as much as if she were his—— Her mind shied away from the word 'mistress' and hastily substituted 'lover'—or 'wife'.

Of course she was over-reacting. After all, she had promised him nothing, least of all her soul.

For the rest of the afternoon Tegan had to use all of her not inconsiderable will-power to keep her mind on her work, and was thoroughly despising herself when she arrived home. By the time she had changed three times scorn had changed to active disgust.

Finally she chose a new dress, its texture and ivory colour complementing her skin. With it she wore opal earrings and a matching ring that had belonged to her grandmother; the brilliant swirls of blue and green and crimson had an exotic, mysterious look.

Was she too elaborately dressed?

From her window she saw the Jaguar come to a stop outside. Too late to think of changing again! Stifling a muffled groan, she gave her hair a final comb to restrain the dark waves, then ran down the stairs to meet him in the foyer.

When Kieran saw her his expression didn't change but he couldn't control the sudden flame in his eyes. Something heated and unmanageable ran through Tegan. She essayed a smile, felt it quiver on her mouth, and wondered despairingly why she didn't just cave in there and then.

'You look like moonlight gardenias,' he said quietly, taking the hand she held out to him and carrying it to his mouth. He kissed it, then drew her towards him while he closed the door behind her.

It was an evening of enchantment. The play lived up to its reputation. Tegan discussed it with him during the interval, over champagne and smoked salmon later, and in the opulent security of the car on the way home, exchanging cool, intellectual observations that belied the sensations raging through her. After that kiss on the hand he hadn't touched her, but once inside the door of her flat he turned her into his arms. His mouth was warm and fierce and demanding, moulding hers beneath it, and that was what she had been waiting for, what she needed.

Her breath sighed into his, mingled; she heard her clock chime, but the time didn't impinge. All she was aware of was his touch, his taste, the male strength of his body against hers, the overwhelming need that arced from her to him and, augmented, sped back again. It was paradise, it was all Tegan ever wanted, and when at last he put her away from him and looked down into her dazed face with heavy-lidded eyes he smiled at the small protesting noise she made.

'I'll see you tomorrow,' he said thickly. 'We'll go out to dinner.'

'I can't.' Her voice was soft and hesitant, almost shocked.

'Why not?'

He had no right to ask, but she explained, 'I'm going out to see a film with a couple of old friends.'

'All right. The next night.'

He didn't even ask, he just told her, and if there was a gleam of defiance in her eyes she knew it faded as soon as they met his, inexorable, hotly possessive.

'All right.' Such compliant surrender was sweet—too sweet. It could become addictive.

And, she thought as she floated into her bedroom after he had gone, her head filled with moonlight and her mouth tender from his kisses, it would be fatally easy to let him walk all over her, to surrender her hard-won autonomy to the intense, driving masculinity, the powerful personality that was Kieran.

The realisation was like a bucket of cold water in her
face, a sudden dousing of her excitement and anticipation. In spite of the smooth, restrained sophistication he
showed the world, Kieran was a primitive, accepting no
rules but his own. He was all dominant male; any relationship, any affair, would be on his terms, not on hers.
If she surrendered to the heat and the need and the devouring passion, lost herself in him, she would no
longer be in control of her life.

In a way it was ironic; men who had wanted more
from her than she was prepared to give called her frigid.
No doubt they would be sourly satisfied if they could
see her humiliating and helpless response to Kieran.

She shivered, remembering how searingly furious he
had been when he'd accused her of exploiting Sam
Hoskings, the words he had flung at her. They had
marked her for life, those insults. And he hadn't really
apologised for them.

Shall we start again? he had asked, then ordered,
Forget I lost my temper.

Not exactly any indication of regret.

Tegan had good reason to be cautious. Carefully
taking off the opals, she turned them slowly so that the
stones shimmered with blue-green flames. Had she
subconsciously chosen them because they were the same
colour as Kieran's eyes?

Prudence told her she should follow her instincts and
have nothing more to do with him, but her rash heart
whispered that that was the coward's way out, and it
was her heart that won.

She was still drifting in a dream when she woke up the
next morning, and the haze of delight stayed with her
all through the day. Perhaps that was why she be-

stowed a radiant smile on Rick Hannibal when he
turned up at Raintree House in the late afternoon.

'Hi,' he said, that pleasant, conspiratorial smile very
much in evidence. 'Is Kieran here? His secretary said he
was out, so I assumed this was where he'd be.'

'Not at the moment, anyway. I haven't got an appointment to meet him here, but he might be planning
to have a look at the place later this afternoon.'

'I think he is. I'll wait and see. You're going to make
a wonderful job of it,' he said enthusiastically. 'I've
seen all the plans and your ideas. You must be extremely clever to have sussed out just what would make
Kieran comfortable.'

Smiling, she inclined her head. 'Thank you, Mr
Hannibal.'

'Oh, Rick, for heaven's sake; I'm not like old Kieran,
so damned formal. I think I'll wait for him, if you don't
mind? Perhaps I could come around with you, see how
you work. Tell me if I get in the way, though.'

'I'm actually on my way back to the office, but the
builders will still be working for another hour, if you
want to wait.'

He grinned. 'They're not as pretty as you,' he said
mournfully and quite outrageously.

Tegan laughed, and he joined in, leaning a little towards her as the sound of their amusement mingled in
the warm air. A movement caught her eye; turning her
head, she saw the silver and green Jaguar come up the
drive.

'Here he is,' she said, anticipation keen as a lance
lighting her eyes to gold.

Kieran was not alone. With him was Andrea, elegant
and erect in the front seat. An identical expression on
the two faces behind the windscreen sent a chill down

Tegan's spine. She walked down the steps, telling herself she didn't need to be so agitated, she hadn't been doing anything to make him suspect her, and, anyway, Kieran had no claim on her...

But when Kieran got out with his usual smooth grace he smiled at them, nothing but cool appraisal in his eyes. 'Were you waiting for us?' he asked.

'I'm on my way back to the office,' Tegan explained, 'but Mr Hannibal was going to wait.'

'Rick,' he complained, helping Andrea from the car. 'I asked you to call me Rick.'

Kieran took Tegan's hand in his. He looked very stern and aloof for a moment, and something subtle and deep inside her quivered. But almost immediately he smiled down teasingly, pleasure gleaming in the crystalline depths of his gaze as he inspected her thoroughly.

Little quivers of excitement tightened her nerves. Her answering smile was oddly tremulous, as though, she thought disgustedly, she were a girl with her very first boyfriend.

'Can you spare the time to walk around with us?' he asked. 'Andrea hasn't seen the house, and I'd like her to have some idea of what it's going to be like.'

She wavered, but when he smiled at her like that she couldn't refuse him. Yet an hour later, when they came out through the front door, uneasiness was chasing in a series of tiny chills up and down her spine. Kieran had spent the entire hour flirting with her. Oh, he wasn't blatant about it—he was too clever for that—but he touched her, and watched her, making sure that the others realised there was more between them than a simple business relationship. He had been almost proprietorial, as though he had been staking a claim.

And that had to be ridiculous, because he didn't feel like that about her. Tegan knew what possessiveness was; Sam had been so resentful of any time she spent away from him that she used to lie about it just to keep the peace. Since then she had become adept at sensing the first flicker of jealousy or acquisitive desire, fleeing any sign with a haste that came close to ruthlessness.

Kieran didn't need her, or want her, like that. She was almost certainly over-reacting, but his attitude left her with an uneasiness that didn't go away, not even when she left them for the refuge of her flat.

Gerald rang before dinner that evening. He was beginning to talk about Blair with a dead, despairing note in his voice that worried Tegan. She promised to go over to their flat the following day.

Narrow brows pleated into a frown, she looked at her watch. An hour before she had to get ready to go the movies. Time enough to do some work.

The latest family at the housing scheme to ask for her help was one of six—a tired mother, a father who worked long hours, and four small children. They had no money, of course, so their project was a real challenge. Smiling, she sat down to make some notes.

Ten minutes later telephone rang again. Sighing, Tegan lifted the receiver and said, 'Hello?' in her most absent voice.

'Darling, if you're as busy as all that I'll hang up!'

'Oh, Mum! No, I'm never too busy to talk to you.' Smiling, she settled down for a chat. Her mother usually rang once a week or so. 'How's the production coming on?' she asked.

Her mother was directing a play for the local amateur dramatic society, and it had been a hard slog.

'I think it's starting to jell at long last,' she said, projecting her enthusiasm in her trained voice.

Tegan smiled, then sobered. Only her mother knew what it had cost her to give up a career that could have led to the heights of stardom in order to become the wife of a doctor in a small, isolated farming and fishing community. Marie Jones had never complained, and during her childhood Tegan had taken her pretty, vivacious mother completely for granted as children did. It was only after she grew up that she began to wonder just how big the sacrifice had been—and how much the lost opportunities still ached.

'We were wondering whether you'd heard any more about Blair?' her mother said.

'Not a word. Mum, Gerald's worrying me. He seems to have given up. He even speaks of her in the past tense now.'

Her mother sighed. 'I suppose it's easier for him to deal with it like that. Keeping hope high is very difficult, very much a strain. And Gerald is not exactly a strong character, is he?'

'You, too?' Tegan muttered, then could have cut out her tongue.

Her mother laughed. 'Someone else thinks he's weak, I gather.'

'Someone else thinks he's a wimp.'

'Dare I ask who the someone else is?'

Tegan smiled. Eagerly looking forward to grandchildren, her mother would dearly love her to find some nice man and marry him. She was, however, far too tactful to press Tegan.

'His name is Kieran Sinclair, and I'm doing a house for him at the moment. He doesn't want me to be doing it; he was a friend of Sam Hoskings's, and he blames me for jilting him.'

'He does, does he?'

Tegan thought with a grin that she could almost feel the antagonism crisping down the line.

Her mother demanded trenchantly, 'Does he know that Sam was busy taking over your life, that he was jealous and dominating, and impossible to deal with, and that you never said you'd marry him anyway?'

Although her mother persuaded Tegan that she couldn't submit to Sam's emotional blackmail, she didn't know of the subsequent scene with Kieran. Only Blair had been told about that, and then only because Tegan had arrived weeping and distraught on her doorstep in the middle of the night.

'No,' Tegan said. 'We don't talk about it.'

'I think you should. There's no reason for him to believe that you were the one at fault.'

Tegan said nothing and after a moment her mother laughed quietly, ruefully. 'All right, I know when to keep quiet. If he doesn't want you to do his house, why are you?'

'Blair was busy with this wretched palace—which will almost certainly come to nothing now—and as Kieran and I had exchanged a few insults after I broke the engagement to Sam I didn't want to work for him. So Alana Richmond, the woman we hired about three months ago, did a scheme, which he didn't like at all. Actually, she did it really well, highlighting his magnificent Regency furniture, but he said it was too trendy, and I can see what he meant. Instead of using the furniture she showcased it, made the pieces *objets d'art*, and Kieran is a man who likes to put his things to the use they were made for.'

'He sounds interesting,' Marie said cautiously.

Tegan nodded. 'Interesting he definitely is.' As well as autocratic, and dynamic and forceful ... 'Anyway, that left me to come up with a design, which I did, and Blair pitched it to him. Fortunately he liked it. He's letting me finish it because he wants to get into the place as soon as possible. He has a contact either in El Amir or close to it, and he's managed to get a few snippets of information, all of which seems to indicate that things are OK, but—oh, Mum, I have this bad feeling.'

'It must be hard, and clearly you're not getting any help from Gerald.'

'No, he's desperate.'

'And the situation with this Kieran Sinclair must be pretty stressful, too.'

'Well, we've agreed to bury the hatchet, so it isn't as difficult as it could be.'

'Who is Kieran Sinclair? The name sounds familiar, but I can't pin a face to it.'

'He's a merchant banker,' Tegan told her, feeling a secret, forbidden pleasure in talking about him.

'Ah, of course.' Her mother's voice was a little faint. 'Is he nice?'

Nice? Well, no, *nice* was not a word that came to mind when she thought of Kieran Sinclair. Fascinating, intriguing, possessed of a dark, smouldering charm that ignited a hidden, desperate need in her—all those! Then she remembered his kindness to Fiona Thompson, the girl he had danced with at the party; yes, niceness was there, somewhere.

'Dangerous,' she said at last, but lightly, because she didn't want her mother to draw any conclusions. 'Not your ordinary man.'

'Are you seeing him?' her mother enquired delicately.

Tegan laughed softly, a note of unconscious yearning underlying her normal crisply confident tones. 'Yes, I suppose so.'

'In that case you had better take care.'

The ring of the doorbell cut the call short. Tegan said a swift goodbye, hung up, and went out into the hall, opening the door to find Kieran standing there.

'Hello,' she said, primeval exultation zigzagging through her.

'I tried to ring, but your number was engaged.'

She nodded, her eyes feasting on him. 'I've been talking to my mother. And before that to Gerald.'

'You can tell him where the information came from,' he said.

Tegan didn't try to hide her surprise. 'Thank you. I think he'd like to know. Although it would be better if you told him.'

'Why?'

'Because you look—oh, competent. No, trustworthy. Oh, I don't know. Believable? Reliable? As though you know what you're talking about?'

He grinned. 'I'm flattered, of course, but I doubt whether my looks convey all that.'

By now she was feeling rather stupid, but she persevered. 'Perhaps the words "merchant banker" have some sort of magic ring. I don't know! Anyway, it's kind of you. I'll tell Gerald tomorrow morning when I see him.'

'You're visiting him?'

She returned his unsmiling look very directly. 'Yes.'

His face was dark and arrogant. 'All right,' he said, as though giving her permission.

Before she had a chance to be indignant he bent his head and kissed her, warmly, persuasively; she had been hungering for it since the previous night. Slowly her arms crept up. She relaxed into his embrace with a sigh of surrender, no longer caring that anyone walking up the stairs to any of the other two flats on her floor could see them.

He smelt of warm male, teasing, aroused, potent with a pagan hunger that sent her brain spinning into unknown regions. Tegan kissed him back, opening her mouth for the thrust of his, giving him all that she could.

When he lifted his head she was breathless, clinging to him. Satisfaction so intense it was like triumph blazed green in his eyes.

'I didn't realise you went in for public lovemaking,' she said huskily, thoroughly antagonised by his blatant reaction.

He smiled, a threat and a promise. 'When I make love to you,' he informed her, touching her lip with a long, lean forefinger, 'everyone in the world will know, because we're going to set it on fire, you and I. I'll see you tomorrow night.'

'Oh?'

'We're going out to dinner, remember?' And he turned and went down the stairs.

Although the evening with her friends was fun, something was lacking. Determined not to become reliant on Kieran for her pleasure, Tegan concentrated hard on the film, and even managed to enjoy drinking coffee and eating cake afterwards.

But when she finally got to sleep she dreamed of Blair, nightmares of imprisonment and abandonment, waking heavy-eyed and listless and worried sick.

The visit to Gerald was every bit as exhausting as she had expected it to be. When she told him that Kieran had told her that so far everything was well with Blair, he cheered up a trifle, but by the time she left he was once more seeing her future in shades of gloom.

Tegan had never before realised how difficult it was to comfort someone who was determined to believe the worst. She probably could have dealt with that, but Gerald's fear and forebodings dragged her own confidence down.

She would have liked to spend longer with him, but that morning she wanted to check out a shop specialising in Oriental imports which had just opened, and after that she had an appointment with a woman who wanted her bedroom redecorated. Shuddering inwardly as she looked around, she agreed that it should be done, and sat down with the client to find out exactly what sort of design she had in mind.

Of course it turned out to be a direct copy of a room in the latest *Vogue*. Without, she hoped, any visible sign of irritation, Tegan began the process of discovering what the woman really wanted, in the process weaning her away from the magnificent but far too opulent room in the photograph. What was perfect for the heart of New York managed to look pretentious and affected in Auckland, with its much less formal life.

Not everyone, she thought wryly as she drove back to the office, had the confidence in their taste that Kieran did.

As she walked past her office, Alana called out, 'Got a moment?'

It was more than a moment, but it was worthwhile. Together they went over estimates for a refurbished sitting-room, then discussed the line of attack for a small but very expensive town house, which was the first commission Alana had been specifically asked to do, and of which, as she said, grimacing, 'I am totally determined not ever to make the same mistake as I did with Sinclair.'

'You won't.' Tegan smiled reassuringly at her as she got to her feet. In her own office the light on the answerphone was flicking. More gloom from Gerald? Lord, she hoped not.

But the voice belonged to Andrea Sinclair. 'Look, can you come and see me this afternoon? I've got some free time then.'

Pulling a face at the autocratic tone, Tegan rang her number.

'Oh, yes, how would two o'clock suit you? I've got an hour or so to fill in.'

Some people, Tegan decided as she mentally rearranged her plans, didn't even know they were being arrogant.

'Yes, that would be fine.'

'Good.' She gave an address that certainly wasn't Kieran's; he had a penthouse on top of one of the new office blocks right in the heart of town, whereas it appeared his sister was living in a very up-market cluster of town houses in one of the eastern maritime suburbs. Several months before, Blair and Tegan had submitted a scheme for one of them, which had been rejected.

Andrea opened the door elegantly dressed in linen trousers and a cream silk shirt, and it was obvious immediately that she was sharing the town house with Rick Hannibal. His briefcase with the tell-tale initials stood on the hall table, and there were other signs of a man's occupancy. So why did Andrea need a bedroom in her brother's house? And what about the other men who hovered around the woman?

Oh, well, Tegan decided, it was no business of hers.

Like her brother, Andrea had definite views on the way her room should look, and the confidence to state them. She also had a professional's eye for detail and quality.

'You don't need me,' Tegan said admiringly. 'You could have done that by yourself.'

Andrea gave her a strange look. 'Do you think so?' The glossy assurance slipped for a moment, to reveal a much softer, more vulnerable woman.

'Yes. That's going to look brilliant, and you know, apart from my telling you where you can get stuff, you've done it all yourself. Have you ever thought of doing this sort of thing as a career?'

The mask clanged back into place. Andrea's brows climbed. 'Hardly,' she said, smiling patronisingly. 'It's just a bit of fun. And I'd find the legwork unutterably boring.'

'Ah, well, if you ever change your mind, let me know. We could use someone with your talent.'

'I doubt whether I'll ever need to work.' Kieran's sister looked around the cool spare room with a faint smile tugging at her beautiful mouth. 'Rick doesn't approve of married women working.'

Now it was Tegan's brows that shot up. 'Really?' she said. 'He sounds a bit like my father. I suppose everyone has different ideas of what work is, anyway. My mother certainly works hard, even though she's never been paid a cent for it. I'd better get going now.'

'Ah, yes, you're going out with Kieran tonight, aren't you?' When Tegan nodded Andrea said thoughtfully,

'He's a hard man, Kieran, but you know that, of course.'

'Yes, I do.'

'When he came back from overseas to take over from our uncles they fought him with everything they could, and they had all the power, but Kieran won after a lot of very public blood-letting. He makes a habit of winning, you see.' She looked sideways at Tegan from beneath her lashes.

Warning her off—but why? Tegan made some noncommittal answer and got herself out of the house, wondering uneasily just what it was about Andrea Sinclair that set her nerves on edge. Had Peter been right when he'd implied she had been a drug addict? If so, it had left her marked, not so much physically as on her soul.

Inevitably Tegan's thoughts drifted to Kieran, and her mouth tucked into a smile. Tonight she would go out to dinner with him, and he would kiss her...

The days that followed were a time of enchantment for Tegan. To her astonishment she discovered they had views in common, and that in spite of his authoritative manner he was prepared to listen when her opinions differed from his, and to discuss them without getting angry or irritated. He certainly stretched her mind, picking on the weakest point of her arguments with unerring accuracy and a keen, slashing intelligence that must make him feared as well as respected.

She hadn't enjoyed matching wits with anyone so much since the heady days of university when the evenings had passed in intellectual bouts that had stimulated and excited her.

Yet the magic was not unalloyed. In the background was the ever-present worry about Blair's welfare. There had been a complete news blackout from El Amir, and even Kieran's bandits in the next little sheikhdom knew nothing about what was going on in the arid mountains where she was held. Tegan spent a lot of time listening to Gerald convince himself that she was dead.

The other source of concern was closer to home. In spite of the intimate dinners at excellent restaurants, the plays, the flight one never-to-be-forgotten weekend across the Tasman Sea to hear a glorious Italian tenor sing his heart out before a rapturously appreciative audience in Sydney's magnificent Opera House, not once did Kieran unleash the passion behind that mask of control.

Tegan thought the night at the opera might be an invitation to his bed, but when he asked her whether she wanted to go he added calmly, 'The arias won't be a prelude to seduction.'

It was then she realised how far down the slippery path of self-delusion she had travelled, for the emotion that filled her was disappointment, pure and simple, mixed with a certain amount of chagrin. Were her feminine attributes so negligible that she couldn't even seduce him after an evening of ravishing music?

Other things worried her. In several of the exclusive restaurants he took her to they had been accosted by people—men who spoke heartily yet deferentially to him, and women who looked at him with avaricious eyes and intimate little smiles. He got rid of them with smooth courtesy, but as the weeks went by Tegan realised that he made no attempt to introduce her to his friends or associates.

At first this seemed a rare and precious compliment. It was plain that he wanted her to himself. Eventually, however, she began to wonder whether there were other, more sinister reasons for such deliberate isolation. Then one night another woman stopped by their table, a woman who made it blatantly plain that she and Kieran had once been lovers.

It was with the utmost difficulty that Tegan kept her expression bland, even a trifle amused, as the woman dropped her voice to a smoky murmur, and let her fingertips trail provocatively along the back of his hand while she played a game of 'Do you remember... ?' more suggestive than either fingertips or voice.

Kieran was polite, but no more.

Perhaps sensing that she was getting nowhere, the woman said, 'And Andrea? Where is she, Kieran? No one seems to know...'

'She's on holiday,' he said, before sending her on her way with a speed and dispatch that Tegan had to admire. Although his ruthlessness made her blink a little, it didn't come close to assuaging the savage jealousy that clawed at her composure and her heart.

'I'm sorry,' he said, as though apologising for an unimportant phone call.

Tegan's eyes were hidden beneath lowered lashes. 'Oh, don't be,' she assured him dulcetly. 'It was an education to see her at work.'

A muscle flicked in his jaw. 'Not one I'd like you to follow.'

Stung, Tegan raised her eyebrows in delicate scorn. 'I don't know,' she said, conscious that she was behaving stupidly but unable to prevent it, 'that your opinion counts for much there. After all, she made it quite

obvious that she was once very much to your liking.
Perhaps I should study her carefully.'

His smile was pure arrogance. 'Not on my account.'

Tegan's chin came up with a speed her parents and
Blair and an assortment of would-be lovers would have
recognised. 'I don't do everything on your account,
Kieran.'

He caught back whatever it was that he had intended
to say and sat looking at her with a hooded gaze that
sent sudden warning bells clanging through her system.
Then he said curtly, 'This, of course, is exactly the result she hoped for by her intrusion, and that grossly
overplayed bit of acting.'

A swift, measuring glance across the room revealed
that, sure enough, there was the other woman watching them, trying unsuccessfully to smother a small,
catlike smile. Tegan leaned towards Kieran, shielding
eyes that glittered with malice beneath a flirtatious
sweep of her lashes. 'I don't like your taste in mis-
tresses,' she said between her teeth.

He picked up her clenched hand and kissed the back
of it. To her fury the taut fingers relaxed as his mouth
worked its magic, sending pulses of sensations through
her.

'Then it's as well you're not my mistress,' he countered, his eyes never leaving hers, boring through the
golden glints of anger to the deep, surging emotions
beneath. 'No, don't look at her; she's not important.
Why do you prickle like hell every time I lay some sort
of claim to you?'

She hesitated, aware that if she answered this she was
propelling their relationship further than she felt comfortable with. Other men had asked the same question,
and been fobbed off; she could not do the same to

Kieran. Her tongue touched her lip. With difficulty she said, 'Independence is important to me. I've had to fight for mine. The harder you fight, the more treasured it becomes.'

He was watching her from beneath lowered lids, his expression impassive. 'Is that why you haven't married?'

'One of the reasons,' she admitted. She searched the angular features of his face, trying to discern whether he took the allusion to Sam, but there was no comprehension there at all.

'And the others?'

She shrugged. They had discussed the world, but their emotions were an area they hadn't covered. She couldn't open that can of worms—not yet, not when he had given her no hint that he understood why she had been forced to reject Sam.

'Too many to talk about unless you've got all night,' she said flippantly. 'Kieran, have you heard anything more from your bandits? Blair's been missing for three weeks now, and nothing seems to be happening about it. Gerald says he can't get any help or comfort from anyone—he even contacted the Red Crescent, but they say they can't get into El Amir, and the news from the country is not good. It looks as though they're in the throes of a full-scale civil war.'

'I'm afraid they are.' The pause that followed made her look up sharply. But all he said was, 'I can't help at all, Tegan.' The closed set of his countenance warned her not to probe further.

CHAPTER FIVE

TEGAN bit her lip. Worry about her friend was a nagging counterpoint to her days. She was suffering from the long hours she was putting in, too.

The news that Decorators Inc was doing Raintree House had brought in a welcome rush of enquiries, all of which Tegan was trying to turn into definite commissions. She had become obsessed with the notion that she had to show Blair a thriving business when she returned.

'You're looking a bit pale,' Kieran said suddenly. 'You're working too hard.'

'I don't think so.'

But when she refused to go out with him that weekend because she had to attend a party given by a woman whose house she had decorated he said impatiently, 'Oh, for heaven's sake, why do you want to go there? She's a silly woman.'

'She's not the brightest of people, I'll grant you that, but she's a dear, and this is a sort of house-warming. She's giving it for me.'

He lifted his brows, his eyes cool and amused. 'Hustling, Tegan?'

The frustration engendered by his distant attitude, and worry about Blair, combined with the hours she had spent since four o'clock that morning working on a proposal, were all taking their toll, but her anger at this remark was sharp and primitive.

'My career is important to me,' she said, keeping her voice level and detached. 'You go out with people you're not all that interested in——'

'At lunchtime,' he said curtly. 'My evenings are my own.'

'What about last Saturday night, when you stayed at your hospitality suite at the tennis tournament with those Malaysian princes? My work is just as important to me as yours is to you.' It was a challenge rooted in the past, she realised even as she flung the words at him, based on the fact that her mother had given up her career, had turned her back on a talent that had never been fulfilled.

She didn't have the same talent, but she was good at her work, she enjoyed it, and she was not going to hear it denigrated by anyone.

'All right.' He surprised her by smiling. 'Ring Wendy Bannister and ask her if you can bring a partner.'

Tegan hesitated. He was watching her from narrowed eyes, the sea-coloured slivers beneath the heavy lashes glinting with challenge. 'You don't want to,' he said softly. 'Ashamed of me, Tegan?'

'No!' But he was right. She didn't want him there, watching her as she trawled delicately, skilfully, for further commissions.

'Then ring Wendy.'

Back at her flat, she reluctantly rang her hostess, who proved to be as generous and open as she always was.

'Of course you must bring a partner,' she said effusively. 'I should have thought of it myself!'

Tegan put the receiver down and turned to face Kieran.

'There,' he said, smiling ironically, apparently not at all bothered by her reluctance. 'It wasn't so hard, was it?'

On Saturday Tegan chose her most striking outfit. It wasn't pretty, exactly; on her fourteenth birthday, when her height had topped five feet eight, she had rejected pretty for inconspicuous. Later, she had worked her way up to striking, with a hiatus after the Sam affair, when she had gone back to inconspicuous again, appalled because he had accused her of deliberately wearing tantalising clothes to enslave him. Now she was back to striking, especially when she was on duty, as she would be that night.

The top in her favourite ivory had a halter-neck that exposed a large part of her elegant, pale gold back, and was eye-catchingly beaded with long strands of crystals and pearls. It revealed sleek satin skin above the waistband of the narrow skirt which was the new shorter length. For decorum she wore the sheerest tights in the same colour as the outfit which flowed almost imperceptibly into pale Italian sandals with a tiny heel.

For a moment she paused, eyeing herself in the mirror. Was there an inordinate amount of skin showing? Her mouth firmed. She was letting Sam's and Peter's comments get under her skin, she thought dismissively. Kieran was far too sophisticated to assume that she wore clothes to cold-bloodedly appeal to men's libidos.

Carefully she applied soft golden-peach lipstick and gold eyeshadow that turned her eyes into large, translucent gold gems, slid outrageously large, dangling fake pearl balls into her ears, and wound another string of pearls and gilt around her wrist. When she had sprayed herself with Chanel No. 5 she looked her reflection over once more. To set off the outfit she had wound her hair in a smooth french pleat that contrasted with its usual exuberance.

Striking, but not vulgar, she decided.

Her appearance brought a glitter to Kieran's eyes, but the thick lashes hid it almost immediately. Kissing her fingers with a touch of European flair, he said, 'Are you dressing for visibility tonight?'

'Yes,' she said simply, her breath catching in her throat at the touch of his mouth on her skin, and the way he looked in the severe black and white of his evening clothes.

'Then you've got it exactly right. You look like a queen of the night—tall and dramatic, with your black hair and pale skin and that shimmery moonlit dress. A cross between an ice maiden and a Valkyrie.'

'I thought Valkyries were large women with long blonde plaited hair and breastplates, who were the rewards for men killed in battle.'

'Valkyries,' he said, 'were extremely dangerous to have around.' He opened the door of the Jaguar and stood back to let her in. 'So was the Queen of the Night—or at least the one in Mozart's opera.'

'That lets me out, then,' she said comfortably. 'I'm not in the least dangerous.'

His smile was amused yet speculative. 'I really think you mean that.'

When they were on their way to the marine suburb that was their destination she said, 'I'm just an ordinary person. You're the dangerous one.'

'It would be interesting,' he said, 'to follow through on this conversation, but let's leave it until after this party, shall we?'

Tegan nodded, and smiled, and looked straight ahead, although her eyes didn't see the traffic.

Anticipation, airy and evanescent, iridiscent as a soap bubble, burgeoned within, colouring her world all the hues of the rainbow.

The Bannisters lived on a cliff-top overlooking the harbour. Their house, built in the Thirties, with its almost windowless back obstinately presented to the magnificent view, had been carefully remodelled to take full advantage of the panorama. Tegan had enjoyed working with Wendy Bannister; she was receptive and fun, and surprisingly discerning when it came to achieving the effect she wanted.

They weren't by any means the first to arrive. The street was full of parked cars, most of them opulent, although there were some interesting elderly ones, rather battered, as well as a superb Rolls-Royce which had to be almost in the veteran class. Wendy might be bubble-headed, but she and her husband came from well-established merchant families.

As Tegan waited for Kieran to lock up she looked around. Although the evening was still and hot there was a faint breeze off the water, carrying with it the scents of gardenias and tuberoses mingled cosily with those of salt and new-mown grass. It was the latter that made her homesick.

She said as much as they walked across the gravel forecourt.

'Homesick for the Coromandel?' Kieran's brows shot up. 'Is there still a country girl tucked inside that very striking urbanite?'

'Alas, you've seen through my disguise.' She shook her head mournfully. 'Actually, for the first twelve years of my life the only time I put on any shoes was when we came up to Auckland to see my grandparents.'

'I won't tell anyone,' he promised, smiling.

Her heart sped into double time. He so rarely gave her that smile, one of complete, unalloyed pleasure without restraint or control. It made her dizzy.

'Oh, Tegan, don't you look super!' Wendy was a small, curvy redhead with a breathless little-girl voice which should have sounded ridiculous on a forty-year-old woman, but didn't, possibly because kindness was one of the most important aspects of her character. 'I wish I had the legs to get away with something like that.' She reached up to kiss Kieran's tanned cheek, ignoring his saturnine smile with aplomb. 'Darling Kieran, trust you to turn up with our clever, talented, stunning Tegan. Even your names match! Celtic to the core. There should be a waiter—ah, there's one. Grab some champagne and mingle, my dears. I don't need to introduce either of you to anyone, do I? You both know just about everyone here.' She beamed impartially at them, made little shooing motions with her hands and went off to take up her position close to the door.

The champagne was delicious. Tegan sipped some then said, trying to sound brisk and confident, 'If you want to circulate without me, I'll understand.'

He looked at her with raised brows and lowered lashes. 'Will you? I'll remember that if I want to. Don't assume I've given you a similar licence.'

The hard note in his voice brought her chin up. 'This is mainly business for me. You'll probably be bored,' she said, turning to greet the architect who had worked with her on the conversion.

Iain Farmer was definitely elevated as he congratulated her on a job well done. 'Darling Tegan!' he enthused, and kissed her with panache. 'We make a great team, you and I, don't we? We should always work together.'

Disentangling herself, she retorted drily, 'Tell me that tomorrow morning when you're sober.'

He laughed, but became instantly respectful when his eyes met those of the man beside her. Glancing at Kieran's still, impassive features, Tegan sighed mentally and introduced them while a chill worked its way through her skin. Surely a man as assured as Kieran didn't suffer from the lack of confidence that had caused Sam's jealousy? He couldn't; it had to be possessiveness, not jealousy, that gleamed like diamond shards in the rich depths of Kieran's eyes.

However, he was perfectly polite to Iain, and to everyone else they met—courteous, polished, producing small talk with an ease that Tegan envied. She had had to learn how to do this, whereas clearly it came naturally to Kieran.

And if she felt a little intimidated by his presence, somewhat cramped by the fact that he clearly intended to spend the entire evening as close to her as possible, well, that was more than offset by the feeling of warm security his presence gave her.

Noting with one part of her brain, the part that was always working, that the house functioned well for a party like this—one of the main points in Wendy's brief—Tegan admitted that behind the shimmering awareness, the scintillating pleasure at being there with Kieran, there was another, more basic emotion. She didn't think she was in love with him, but she was poised on the brink. If she had any sense she'd finish it soon, before she was really hurt. Love exacted too much in the way of payment, and she wasn't prepared to stand the cost.

But she knew she wouldn't tell him to go.

'Darlings,' Wendy enthused as she came up leading a couple. 'Here are Sylvia and Don Spain, who are looking for a decorator. They love this house, and they were really interested when I told them that Tegan is doing your house too, Kieran.'

She beamed at them all, convinced that she had done Tegan a good turn. Unfortunately it soon became clear that the Spains were angling for a closer acquaintance with Kieran, and had decided that a conducted tour of his house might be one way of managing this. Ice began to collect in Tegan's veins. She didn't even need to look at Kieran to realise that such a visit, although freely offered by many proud home owners, was not on his agenda.

She had to use all her tactical skills to avoid being put in a position where she'd have to make a direct refusal, and although she sensed their disappointment she finally managed to do it, fobbing them off with the promise to show them several other houses she had worked on.

'Tegan is a dream to work with, and a darling to boot!' Wendy assured them as she drew them away. 'And so talented—well, you can see from this place! Now, come and meet some people who are just dying to be introduced...' She bustled the Spains off, bestowing a conspiratorial wink over her shoulder at Tegan.

Tegan cringed. Waiting until they were out of earshot, she said, 'I'm sorry about that,' adding defensively, 'I did tell you you'd probably be bored.'

'I wasn't exactly bored.' But he sounded cynical, almost jaded. 'It was a privilege to watch someone net so skilfully for a couple of elusive fish.'

Gold glittered balefully for a second in her eyes, until her sense of humour came to her rescue. 'You can return the privilege one day. I'd like to see you banking.'

'You won't see me prostitute myself,' he said savagely. 'I suppose I should be thankful that you didn't use me as your pimp. Don't *ever* show anyone around my house. I do not want it used as a teaser to persuade someone to use your services.'

Tegan's breath stopped in her throat, clogged into a lump in her chest. For a moment she stared at his inexorable face, then she turned and started blindly across the room.

Cruel fingers at her waist stopped her. 'Smile,' he ordered, *sotto voce*, as a voice she recognised said on a note of surprise,

'Kieran! Fancy meeting you here.'

Andrea Sinclair. Tegan froze, aware of the leashed tension in the big body that was shielding her shocked face from the rest of the room. Blinking suddenly wet lashes, she forced her expression to mimic some sort of welcome as she glanced up.

There was certainly no hint of antagonism in the smile he gave his sister as she stopped beside them, clad in a jumpsuit that had to be pure silk, its sleek, skin-tight contours barely hidden by a diaphanous silk shirt.

'I shouldn't have thought this was your style at all,' Andrea said, her smile not warming her expression. 'But I suppose all of us do things for others we wouldn't do for ourselves.' Mockery gleamed in the large, carefully made-up eyes. Andrea Sinclair looked limpidly from Tegan's still face to her brother's arrogant one. 'Becoming domesticated?' she asked him. 'Or are you a trophy, I wonder?'

Tegan stiffened, but Kieran gave his sister a slow, lazy smile and said lightly, 'Neither. Are you here alone, or is Rick around somewhere?'

'He's lurking about.' She gave a soft, meaningless laugh and airily waved a slender hand. 'Just look for a thundercloud.'

Kieran didn't say anything and his sister's smile wavered. 'Yes, we've had another fight. You know, love is hell, isn't it? I can't think why I bother.'

Her speech wasn't slurred, but something in the way she spoke made Tegan wonder whether she'd had just a little too much to drink.

'He's on his way across the room,' Kieran said curtly.

Rick Hannibal was not so adept as Kieran at hiding his feelings. He arrived wearing a frown that dissipated only when he looked at Tegan.

'Hello,' he said, leaning forward slightly. 'How nice to see you. You know, that outfit is the most astonishing thing I've ever seen. I've been watching you sparkle and glitter in it across the room; if you wanted to attract attention, you certainly went the right way about it. I could hardly take my eyes off you.'

Andrea turned on her heel and walked away, every line in her back expressing fury. Rick stared after her before saying with every appearance of amazement, 'What have I done now?'

But there was enough muted satisfaction in the younger man's voice for Tegan to understand that he had deliberately infuriated Andrea. She didn't answer; this had nothing to do with her, and judging by the cold angularity of Kieran's face she would do well to keep out of it.

'Will you both excuse me for a few minutes?' she said firmly. 'I've seen someone I need to talk to.'

As she walked away she had the disconcerting feeling that neither man even noticed her departure.

She stayed away for the next hour, obscurely threatened by the fact that Kieran was extremely popular; everybody seemed to want to talk to him. Tegan drifted around, talking and making new acquaintances, keeping her eyes carefully averted from that part of the room where he held court. It was difficult. Sooner or later her wayward gaze was drawn back to his darkly powerful figure.

However, by dint of concentration and self-control she managed to look at him only a few times. It was unnerving to find that each time he was watching her. Their gazes clashed for a silent, taut second.

Andrea was enjoying herself in the centre of a group of mainly men. The laughter emanating from it seemed to indicate that everyone there was having a magnificent time. Tegan wandered out on to the terrace at the back of the house, coming to a dismayed halt when she realised that the only other person looking out over the moonlit reaches of the harbour was Rick Hannibal.

'Hello,' he said, setting his glass down. 'Come and join me. Lovely night, isn't it? Pity we've both been deserted by our respective Sinclairs. Never mind; sit down and finish that glass you've been nursing for the last hour. There won't be any bubbles left if you don't drink it soon, and champagne without the bubbles is only boring white wine, you know. We can entertain ourselves by discussing the habits and habitat of those most intriguing creatures, the Sinclair siblings. I must say, yours seems almost tame tonight.'

'I gather you've had a quarrel.' The raw note of pain in his voice plucked at Tegan's sympathy.

'I don't quarrel.' He picked his glass up and took another large swallow. 'I'm a placid soul. Just as well. Andrea looks like a delicate little flower, easily bruised and battered by the weather, doesn't she? Fragile and charming and sensitive. Which is surprising when you think of it, because she can bruise and batter with the best of storms.'

Surprised, as much by his matter-of-fact tone as by his words, Tegan said, 'Quarrels are always awful.'

'Aren't they just!' He gave her a lop-sided smile. 'Take my advice, Tegan Jones, and have nothing to do with the Sinclairs. They don't think the same way as the rest of humanity. That's what happens when you grow up believing that the world's sole function is to do as you say and keep out of your way. They look like something heroic from the days when men fought dragons and women were the prize, but like all anach——' his tongue stumbled over the word, but he caught himself up swiftly '—anachronisms they're out of place in this very unheroic day and age. So they give everyone, especially their nearest and dearest, hell.'

'I'm sorry you're feeling wretched. But you know you're going to feel worse tomorrow morning if you keep drinking and wallowing in self-pity.'

'Ouch!' In the moonlight his smile was pained and self-derisory. 'That sounds as though you could be tough enough to cope with big brother. Good for you. It's time some woman gave him hell; he's had it too easy since he seduced his first woman. If I remember correctly, he was about fourteen at the time. In that case, perhaps she seduced him. What's that scent?'

'Tobacco flowers,' she told him, trying hard to keep the shock from her voice. 'Mixed with Queen of the Night, I think.'

Free Books! Free Prizes!
1, 2 and 3 on the other

▼ CAREFULLY PRE-FOLD & SEPARATE

"WIN-A-FORTUNE" GAME!

HERE'S HOW TO ENTER

1 Play the WIN-A-FORTUNE Tickets on the front of this game piece to enter the Million Dollar Sweepstakes. If one of your unique sweepstakes entry numbers is a winner and you return this game piece, you could win the amount revealed under the scratch-off–even the $1,000,000.00 Grand Prize! (SEE RULES IN BACK OF BOOK FOR DETAILS.)

2 Play the LUCKY 7 SLOT MACHINE to get free Harlequin Presents® novels. The books are yours to keep absolutely free. We'll send them as your introduction to the Harlequin Reader Service®, but no purchase is necessary, now or ever!

3 Play the ACE OF HEARTS game to get a free mystery gift along with your free books!

4 Write your name and address below, detach this entire reply form and return it in the reply envelope provided!

106 CIH ANR4
(U-H-P-04/94)

_____
Name

_____
Address

_____
City   State   Zip

NO PURCHASE NECESSARY—
ALTERNATE MEANS OF ENTRY

To enter the Million Dollar Sweepstakes without requesting the free books and mystery gift, play the Win-A-Fortune game only. Or you may hand print "Win-A-Fortune" plus your name and address on a 3"x5" card and send it to: Million Dollar Sweepstakes (III), P.O. Box 1867, Buffalo NY 14269-1867, and we'll assign sweepstakes numbers to you. LIMIT: One entry per envelope. See rules in back of book for complete details. But why not get everything being offered! After all, the Books and Gift are ABSOLUTELY FREE—yours to keep and enjoy with no obligation to buy anything, now or ever!

1

3 WAYS TO PLAY

for big CASH prizes and FREE GIFTS!
First play your "Win-A-Fortune" game tickets
to qualify for up to

See inside

ONE MILLION DOLLARS IN LIFETIME INCOME
– that's $33,333.33 each year for 30 years!

WIN A CASH **F** **RTUNE**

GAME TIX NO.
1a

Game Ticket values vary. Scratch GOLD from Big Money
Wheel to determine the potential cash value of prize you will
receive if this ticket has a prizewinning sweepstakes number.

YOUR EXCLUSIVE
LUCKY NUMBER IS   2H394131

DO NOT SEPARATE—KEEP ALL GAMES INTACT

WIN A CASH **F** **RTUNE**

GAME TIX NO.
1b

Game Ticket values vary. Scratch GOLD from Big Money
Wheel to determine the potential cash value of prize you will
receive if this ticket has a prizewinning sweepstakes number.

YOUR EXCLUSIVE
LUCKY NUMBER IS   7A278607

DO NOT SEPARATE—KEEP ALL GAMES INTACT

WIN A CASH **F** **RTUNE**

GAME TIX NO.
1c

Game Ticket values vary. Scratch GOLD from Big Money
Wheel to determine the potential cash value of prize you will
receive if this ticket has a prizewinning sweepstakes number.

YOUR EXCLUSIVE
LUCKY NUMBER IS   4R661488

DO NOT SEPARATE—KEEP ALL GAMES INTACT

WIN A CASH **F** **RTUNE**

GAME TIX NO.
1d

Game Ticket values vary. Scratch GOLD from Big Money
Wheel to determine the potential cash value of prize you will
receive if this ticket has a prizewinning sweepstakes number.

YOUR EXCLUSIVE
LUCKY NUMBER IS   6U373305

DO NOT SEPARATE—KEEP ALL GAMES INTACT

WIN A CASH **F** **RTUNE**

GAME TIX NO.
1e

Game Ticket values vary. Scratch GOLD from Big Money
Wheel to determine the potential cash value of prize you will
receive if this ticket has a prizewinning sweepstakes number.

YOUR EXCLUSIVE
LUCKY NUMBER IS   9K512161

DO NOT SEPARATE—KEEP ALL GAMES INTACT

◄ FOLD ALONG DOTTED LINE AND DETACH CAREFULLY ◄

Wendy had intended this terrace to be used after dark, insisting that the landscaper plant shrubs and flowers that scented the night air. It was a pity the party had stayed obstinately inside tonight.

'Oh?' His laughter ghosted on the air. 'Come and sit down, tell me all about yourself. Andrea's as curious as hell about you, did you know that? She doesn't know what Kieran sees in you, but by God I do. She's beautiful, but you're—you stick in the memory, like a vision of delight. Forbidden—tantalising—with hidden, exciting depths that make any man want to find out how far they can go. Not that I can tell her that, of course. One thing you'll find out about the Sinclair siblings is that they are very posh—possessive. They might not exactly want you for themselves, but there's a hint of the dog-in-the-manger about them.'

'Rick——' she began feeling enormously sorry for him and exasperated at the same time. A cold, incisive voice interrupted her.

'Leave him to his drinking,' Kieran said evenly. 'It's time we left.'

Rick lifted his glass in a toast. 'Enjoy yourselves, my children,' he said, slurring the words a little.

'Don't you drive home.' It was an order, delivered in a flat, expressionless voice.

Rick laughed bitterly. 'No, I won't drive. We came in a taxi and we'll go home in a taxi. Don't worry, I won't hurt your precious sister.'

Hard fingers clamped on to Tegan's bare arm, sending shudders through her. 'Let's go,' Kieran said.

Just inside the house they were met by Wendy, still ebullient, still enjoying her party immensely. 'Oh, Tegan, it's absolutely wonderful! If you knew how many years I've been dreaming of a place like this, so easy to entertain in! You clever, clever girl! It's everything I ever wanted, or dreamed of!'

Gushing such enthusiasm might be, but Tegan was not proof against it. Her face lit up as she smiled down at her hostess. 'I'm so glad,' she said simply.

Wendy twinkled. 'I've been singing your praises for months, so with any luck you'll get some commissions out of it all,' she confided. 'Oh, Kieran, you're not going yet, surely? Nigel's just putting some music on; why don't you ask Tegan to dance?'

'No, thank you,' he said smoothly. 'I think it's time we left. I'm expecting a call from overseas that I need to answer myself.'

Wendy twinkled some more. It was clear that she didn't believe a word of it, envisaging a far more romantic reason for their departure. 'In that case, of course I won't keep you. Goodnight,' she called with a knowing intonation, waving as they walked down the front steps.

Tegan shivered.

Kieran had been looking straight ahead but he said instantly, 'You should have worn a jacket.'

She shrugged. 'I'm not really cold, it's just—oh, a goose ran over my grave.'

He looked her over, his teeth gleaming in a sudden, menacing smile. 'I wasn't exactly thinking of how cold you are likely to be. All that delectable skin is too much of an invitation. Didn't you notice the looks of startled appreciation you were getting all evening?'

She stiffened. Deliberately misunderstanding, she said, 'This is as safe an area as any you'll get in Auckland.'

'No area, not even a monastery, could be considered safe when you wear that,' he said.

Every tiny hair on her body lifted. 'Thank you,' she said shortly. 'I think.'

There was something different about his expression, something she distrusted. After letting his gaze wander in a leisurely fashion over her he said mildly, 'You don't think that you may be sending out the wrong signals? I presume when you go out hustling you expect your prospective clients to treat you as a professional? If that's the impression you want to make, wearing clothes like that would seem to be counter-productive.'

She bit off a sudden, horrified gasp. His accusations about her prostituting herself for the business were still burned on to her brain, but she fought down the instant fury and indignation. The angry allegations were too closely allied to the insults he had flung at her after the fiasco with Sam for her to be able to deal with them now. She needed time to reflect, time, she realised, to decide whether his attitude precluded any sort of future for them. She certainly wasn't going to risk her well-being on a man who saw her as a harlot.

Though, to be honest, she could see what he meant. The awful Spains had dangled the possibility of a commission in front of her as bait to ease them into Kieran's house, and, possibly, his social life.

'In this business,' she said, trying to hide her outrage and pain under a cloak of objectivity, 'some sort of flash and dazzle is almost necessary. It's rather like being an actress—people expect you to be a little over-the-top. And I have established my reputation as a decorator. Ultimately, that's why people hire me. The clothes are just the glitter on the ribbon.'

There, that should tell him that she was a professional, with an image and reputation which were important to her. The hoary old chestnuts of sleeping one's way into contracts were still tossed around, but surely by now he knew her well enough to understand that she was not like that.

'Even though you look like something from a man's feverish dream of paradise?'

Tegan's heart jumped in her breast but she retained enough composure to say quietly, 'I think you're exaggerating. Your own sister was wearing something much more spectacular.' She had been going to say provocative, but caution prompted the substitution. Kieran's attitude towards his sister was not easy to fathom, but there was definitely a protective streak in him.

They reached the wide gates, open now. Apart from the whisper of muted music in the air it was very quiet. Often a sea-breeze mitigated the oppressive humidity of nights such as this, but the tentative beginning of one had died with the moonrise, leaving an atmosphere that was heavy and close.

When they reached the footpath Kieran automatically stepped to the road side. With eyes almost accustomed to the dark, Tegan followed as she noticed shapes along the road, shapes that moved. A sharp noise, followed by a muffled voice, brought her to a sudden stop.

Kieran's hand on her shoulder was followed almost simultaneously by the hard forcefulness of the other one over her mouth. Without giving her any option he turned her and lifted her into the shelter of a three-metre-tall pohutukawa tree on the grass verge in a single smooth, powerful, silent movement. He held her clamped against the hard tension of his body as they both listened. No further sound broke through the warm night, but down the road at least two outlines, more solid against the darkness of a high hedge, gave themselves away by their movements.

'Mff!'

'Shut up.' Kieran's voice was barely audible, a mere thread of sound. 'Understand?'

She nodded vigorously. His hand fell away from her lips. Are they breaking into the cars? she mouthed.

'Yes. Get back inside and warn them,' he murmured. 'If anyone touches you, or you hear a noise, scream at the top of your lungs. Go *on*, damn you.'

He turned, pushing her towards the gates, then set off down the road, running with a lethal, prowling gate that sent shivers down her spine. After a moment's horrifying hesitation, Tegan followed orders and set off as silently as she could for the house. Halfway across the forecourt she met a couple.

'Someone's doing over the cars,' she muttered urgently. 'At least two, possibly three people. Go back and ring the police, and get as many men as you can out here. Quickly, please—Kieran's gone to stop them!'

Then she turned back. Big and strong as Kieran was, he wasn't Superman.

A yell made her sprint, long legs flashing. Thank heavens she wasn't wearing high heels. It hadn't sounded like Kieran's voice, but her heart was thudding so much that she might not have recognised it.

She skidded to a halt as a man arced back through the air before landing with a nasty thick thud on the footpath, where he lay twitching with two others. Tegan's heart leapt as she recognised Kieran's silhouette. His hands fell to his sides. When she tried to say his name she discovered that fear and adrenalin had dried her mouth and only a croak came forth. She wasn't expecting the speed with which he whipped around.

'It's all right,' she gasped, weak with relief as she heard people running from the house. 'It's me.'

'I thought I told you to go inside and tell them what was happening.' He was breathing heavily but certainly not from exhaustion.

Tegan looked from him to the three men who sprawled on the ground. How on earth had he managed to lay them all out?

'I did tell someone,' she snapped, the adrenalin-rush making her feel sightly ill. 'I came back in case you needed some help.'

When he started to laugh she could have hit him, so furious was she. One of the men on the ground moved, his hand groping out. Kieran set his foot on a sinewy wrist—not heavily, but the casual imprisonment was a threat that the man understood. He lay still.

By then reinforcements had arrived, and Tegan was submerged in the general hubbub.

An hour later the three battered thieves had been driven off, statements taken, and Tegan was sitting in the front seat of the Jaguar listening to Kieran say with cold deliberation, 'If you ever disobey me again like that, I'll——'

'I did what you told me to,' she countered heatedly. 'I told someone.'

'And then you came back. Of all the stupid, hare-brained things to do——'

'I didn't know whether you'd be able to manage them. I was almost certain there were three of them, and I was worried! How was I to know you were an expert at unarmed combat?'

'I wouldn't have tried to stop them if I hadn't been confident I could cope. I'm not a hot-headed young kid with a name to make. But you put yourself in danger! In clothes that are open incitement to riot——'

'For the last time,' she said between her teeth, 'there's nothing wrong with this outfit! It's perfectly decent, more decent than a lot that were at the party tonight. Stop being so stuffy and tell me why you went off to attack those idiots instead of doing the sensible thing and waiting for someone to come and help you deal with them.'

They reached her flat. He swung the car into the kerb and switched off the engine. 'They were leaving,' he said curtly as he got out.

'Then you should have let them go.' Without waiting for him to let her out she strode across the footpath and inserted her key in the main door with a stabbing motion.

'Why?'

Her snort probably echoed up the stairs. 'Because that's what you're *supposed* to do, that's why. The police always say don't put yourself in danger, contact them.'

'If I'd done that,' he said reasonably, 'they'd have been long gone by the time the police got there, and so would the pile of stuff they'd stolen. I'm not an idiot, Tegan; I know how many men I can deal with, and these were well within my capabilities, believe me. I had a good look before I decided I could take them.'

'But why? Why did you do it?'

'Because I happen to believe that it's our responsibility to help the forces of law and order as much as each of us is able to.'

Her long legs took the stairs in a near-run. It sounded logical, but all she could think of was that he might have been hurt. Unlocking her front door with a vicious twist of her wrist, she said, 'That sounds great, and I'm all for it, but what if they'd had weapons?'

He pushed her door open and went in before her, effortlessly dominating the hall and the sitting-room. 'I know my own limitations,' he said.

Something in his voice made her demand sharply, 'Did they have weapons? Kieran, tell me!'

His glance was opaque, enigmatic. 'One had a knife,' he admitted slowly. 'He was pretty clumsy with it, though.'

Tegan's eyes widened enormously. She took a step towards him, searching the hard, dark face for signs of wounds. 'He didn't hurt you, did he?' she breathed, appalled.

'No. I said he was clumsy.' He smiled, genuine amusement gleaming in the blazing aquamarine depths of his glance, amusement that hid a purpose she barely noticed, although a slight shudder touched her skin with an eerie fingerprint.

'Oh, God,' she almost wailed. 'You great idiot!'

'Tegan, they were useless, just rank amateurs.'

'But a knife——'

'He didn't know how to use it,' he said soothingly and bent to kiss her forehead.

Tegan clung. He could have been killed, and she would have been desolate for the rest of her life. It was no longer a question of whether she could pull back from the brink; she already loved this maddening, unknowable man, with his lethal skills and toughness, his brain and his sophistication. A sob broke through. She gulped it down, but she couldn't control the next one.

'Don't you ever do that again,' she mumbled, hiding her head in his chest. 'You fool; I should—I should——' Hiccuping, she choked back the tears.

'It's all right,' he murmured, holding her gently, too gently. 'It's just the adrenalin catching up with you. Cry and get it out of your system.'

'Shut up!' she said on a muffled sob, and pulled his face down and kissed him with a desperate, famished hunger, as though this were the end, there were never going to be another tomorrow.

He responded just as ferociously, straining her against the hard perfection of his body. By now she knew him intimately—the way his chest moved when he drew in a breath, the contours, flowing, masculine, lithe, of his body. He was exceptionally tall, but there was nothing shambling about him, none of the slowness that so often accompanied very tall people. He was perfectly proportioned, sleek and vital and strong. Heaven was in his arms, in his mouth.

'I'm sorry.' He had lifted his head, but spoke against her mouth. 'I hurt you.'

'No.' Her lips were tingling, but the sensations that rioted through her set that at nought.

'You go to my head like good wine,' he said raggedly.

She guided his head closer, fitted her mouth to his and once more took the initiative, her sensuality unleashed by the events of the night and her sudden, shocking recognition of her true emotions.

He kissed her with an uncurbed passion, his hands pulling her hips into the cradle of his so that she felt the evidence of his desire. Always before she had been slightly repelled by a man's open arousal, but not this time. This time she moved against him with an innocent abandon, trembling with the new and exciting sensations this produced throughout her body.

'Tegan,' he said harshly.

Her heart roaring in her ears, she opened her mouth to the invasion of his, luring him in with a provocation that came naturally, although she had never done anything like this before. His skin was hot, like fire, and the hardness of his body and the heat of it, the scent of his masculinity in her nostrils, the abrupt thrust of his tongue into her mouth, acted on her emotions like an incitement to riot.

At last he sighed, and pushed her away. 'My hands are shaking,' he said drily. 'I'll see you tomorrow.'

Her head was clouded, filled with the fumes of passion. 'Tomorrow?'

He laughed softly beneath his breath. 'Tomorrow. Remember, you're going to pick me up at three to take me to the man who's going to repair the staircase.'

Not hearing, she nodded, her eyes fixed on his face. 'You don't have to go home now, do you?'

He groaned and pulled her into his arms again, not kissing her, just holding her against him so that she could feel the need in him.

Tegan turned her face into his throat, kissing the fine-grained skin, delicately tasting its salty flavour, breathing deeply so that she savoured his very essence with a gourmet's fastidious delight. More than anything she wanted to lie with him between tangled sheets and give herself to him, take him, lost to the world in a rapture such as she had never known. She began to shiver, unable to control the desire that held her in thrall.

'It's all right,' he murmured, pressing little kisses against her temple and down the smooth sweep of her cheekbone. 'It's all right, Tegan. Calm down.'

'I want you too much,' she said beneath her breath.

He was very still. Then a hand under her chin tilted her head so that he looked down into her eyes, his own clear and sharp as a raptor's intense gaze. 'Do you?'

'Yes, damn you!'

The hand beneath her chin slid down her throat, lingering on the soft, stretched length, found the smooth skin below, and still moving leisurely, deliberately, cupped the high thrust of a breast.

'And damn you, too,' he said conversationally, watching as she stiffened to combat the flood of enervating languor that submerged her will-power.

Unexpectedly his thumb flicked across the pouting nipple. The crystal beads jangled like tiny bells. Assailed by heat and need, Tegan gasped, then bit her lip to keep a slow moan back as he did it again.

'Don't,' she whispered, shuddering with pleasure.

'Why not?'

'Because I don't know what to do...'

He stopped as though the answer surprised him. Then he said quietly, 'You say yes, my spirited Tegan, my Celtic goddess. That's what you do.'

She said thickly, 'You know I want to.'

'Then say it.'

She lifted her head, scanning the drawn angles of his face in the mellow golden light of the lamp, the pattern of light and shade, savage, formidable. An atavistic chill ran down her spine. He wanted nothing less than total surrender.

CHAPTER SIX

'AND you?' she asked, trying to think, trying to organise her thoughts and emotions into some logical sequence. 'What do you say?'

He gave a twisted, ironic smile. 'That I've wanted you from the first moment I saw you. But you knew that already. Wanting is easy; it's as instinctive as breathing and eating and laughing. Now I know you, and this is much more than merely wanting.'

It was what she wanted to hear, what she needed to hear. No passionate, florid declaration of love could have meant more at that particular moment.

'Yes,' she said simply, touching his top lip with her finger.

'Just like that?'

She nodded, and he gave a muffled groan, and bent to kiss her once more, fiercely, passionately, but only for a few seconds.

'I have to go,' he said inexorably. 'I really am expecting an important call in half an hour, and the shadows under your eyes tell me that you need to sleep. I'll be busy in the morning, but I'll pick you up at three tomorrow, and we'll talk then.'

Excitement, and a variety of wholly unnecessary qualms, kept Tegan awake for some time after she went to bed, but eventually exhaustion intervened and she slept, to wake late and reluctantly to a lethargy she recognised as only partly physical. For a moment she was tempted to give in to it.

'Don't be a coward,' she commanded herself, and got out of bed and went for a brisk walk down to the Rose Gardens.

Blair loved roses; each year about this time they had a picnic in the Gardens, and went around solemnly smelling each variety, awarding them a mark out of ten. Tegan smiled as she remembered the fuss last year when Blair had been stung on the nose. Gerald had panicked, but after the first moments spent spluttering and swearing Blair had laughed.

Where was she now? Still in those arid mountains, more or less a prisoner, wondering whether she was ever going to be released?

Tegan turned away from the beds of flowers. Somehow she didn't feel like staying there.

Just outside the Gardens a car slowed down as it went past, then pulled sharply over and stopped. Preparing to deliver a blistering reproof to the driver, Tegan realised that the man who got out and walked down the footpath towards her was Rick Hannibal.

'Hello,' she said warily. He looked terrible, with dark circles under his eyes as though he hadn't slept all night.

'Hi. Can I give you a lift?'

She shook her head. 'No, I'm chasing a few cobwebs away.'

He pushed his hand through his hair. 'Are you in a hurry?'

'N-no. Not really.'

'Then can I talk you into have a cup of coffee with me?' The bright umbrellas and flowers of a popular restaurant that served breakfasts caught his eye. 'Giorgio's is good, I believe.'

When Tegan hesitated he gave her a coaxing, cajoling smile that didn't quite hide the bleakness. It was that glimpse into a private hell which made her say, 'Yes, I'd like that.'

Ensconced at an outside table, one that overlooked the soft brilliance of the roses in the Gardens, he ordered coffee and orange juice and croissants. There were others in the restaurant, although no one Tegan recognised. In spite of the fact that he didn't seem to know anyone there either he chose a slightly secluded table behind a row of flowering bougainvillaea in pots.

They talked of the party the night before until the food and coffee arrived. Then apropos of nothing, he asked, 'Was Kieran angry last night?'

'No. Why should he be?'

Shrugging moodily, Rick piled two spoonfuls of sugar into his coffee. 'Oh, just that he found us talking together in the dark. He's possessive.'

'He might be, but he's not unreasonable,' she returned tartly.

He laughed at that, then grimaced like a child caught out in mischief. 'You've got a lot to learn. Of course he's unreasonable. That's why he's got so far—he just refuses to admit the possibility of defeat, so it doesn't happen.'

'I don't know that I'd call that unreasonable,' she objected.

'Because he's the man he is? Determined and confident? Perhaps. How about this, then? I have it on the best authority that the reason he broke off his engagement was because the woman wouldn't give up her job and settle down to be a good Sinclair wife and mother. In this day and age, that's unreasonable.'

Tegan tried to be fair. Ignoring a pang of outraged jealousy, she said, 'No one can know what makes an engagement go sour, what happens inside a relationship.'

'Unless one of them spills the beans. Her name is Kirsty MacDonald, and she came up for a week a while ago. She and Andrea had a good old night's letting-down of hair, and she told us what had gone wrong. She was quite frank about it. She's a stockbroker and Kieran said that unless she gave up her career it was all off. She was shattered. She's still carrying a torch for him, because she came up to see whether they could make another go of it, but he wasn't having any.' He drank some of his coffee. 'She's beautiful, and witty, and intelligent, and she knows how to behave, so he must have dumped her because she wouldn't give up her job. Now, that is completely unreasonable.'

'Yes, it is, if that's all that the engagement foundered on. He can't have loved her.'

Rick laughed discordantly. 'I don't think they know how to love,' he said. 'Sex, now, that's different. When she was in her cups the beauteous Kirsty was rather embarrassingly open about Kieran's prowess as a lover, and Andrea——' He stopped, looking ashamed. 'Sorry, I didn't mean to—forget I ever said that, will you?'

'Yes, of course.' She was busy fighting back a black flood of fury at the thought of Kieran making love to another woman.

'Anyway, it's all over. I'm not going to hang around to be made look a fool. I've left Andrea.'

Tegan gave him a startled look. 'I'm sorry,' she said a little tentatively.

'Are you?' He gave a defiant, mirthless smile. 'Well, if you aren't now you soon will be, because it means you'll have her on your back all the time. She's completely reliant on Kieran for emotional support. Which makes life bloody hard for her lovers. There's no room for them in her life except as studs, and in spite of folklore most men find it just as degrading to be a sex object as it is for a woman. Whenever things don't go her way Andrea runs to Kieran. He's always been there for her, and he's such a bloody paragon, how can I compete? I'm getting out. I'm going to England. She's always telling me I should get some sophistication, so I'll do that, and when I come back home I might be able to look at her without loving her.'

'She sounds,' Tegan said quietly, 'pretty unlovable.'

He frowned at an inoffensive croissant. 'No, she can be—oh, forget it. She's got problems. I thought I could help her, but she's the only one who can deal with them, and as long as she's got big brother to shepherd her through she's not going to even try. Sorry I'm being such a bore. I'd better take you home.'

Back at home she couldn't settle to work. Rick's revelations had hit her on a particularly sore spot. Passion was one thing—she had wanted men before, although never like this, she thought, biting her lip as the slow fires heated her blood—but love was another thing entirely.

She was afraid of love. Love had made Sam totally irrational and arbitrary, so that in the end he had seemed to resent even the breath she took. Love had persuaded her mother to give up a career that promised acclaim and satisfaction, a rare sense of accomplishment. Tegan had read the scrapbooks that documented the young Marie Thornton's progress as an actress, and the plaudits in the yellowed scraps of newspaper had made her wonder what on earth Marie had seen in her father to turn her back on such prospects.

Her father, too, had been jealous. The scrapbooks were a secret she shared with her mother. The only row she could remember them having was when her mother had decided to revive the moribund local dramatic society. Even to the fourteen-year-old child she had been it was obvious that her father feared that a mere taste of the stage might be enough to lure his wife back to the old life. Would she end up like that, a lesser being because she loved?

If Kieran asked her to give up her career, would she do it?

She collapsed bonelessly into a chair, and began drumming her fingers on the arm as she stared at the rug on the floor until the gentle apricot and cream pattern danced and reformed in her eyes. All right, so it wasn't a vocation like her father's and she didn't have a rare and brilliant talent like her mother. Making lovely interiors perhaps didn't help humanity all that much. Not like Kieran, with his venture capital invested in mankind's future. But she gave people immense pleasure, and surely that counted for something!

Wendy's radiant face popped into her mind. Her talent and skill had provided Wendy with a house that would add to her happiness, a setting that would lift her spirits. Tegan was profoundly affected by her surroundings, by landscapes, by colours. She believed that most people were, far more than they realised.

That was why she spent time she could ill afford with families who lived in state houses, helping them use their meagre budgets to the best advantage. People had the right to live in places that increased their pleasure in life.

If Kieran wanted her to give up her work, would she?

He hadn't asked, she told herself ruthlessly. He didn't say anything about marriage. He hasn't even said he loves you. He probably doesn't.

More than wanting, he'd said. This is more than wanting.

Of course it could merely mean that he liked her. If that was so she was in trouble, because she didn't just like him—she loved him with such passion, such need for him, that it terrified her.

What did that surrender she had given him mean? An agreement to an affair, something ephemeral, based only on passion, and when it was over a goodbye said without emotion?

'I must have been mad!' she whispered into the quiet serenity of her room. A siren warbled somewhere in the distance, an ambulance ferrying a casualty to hospital. A shiver ran down her spine as she recalled the way Kieran had dispatched the three thieves so easily, almost nonchalantly, the night before. She wasn't afraid he'd use his strength against her, but something about his calm victory sent warnings racing through her mind.

This afternoon, she decided quickly, she would tell him that she didn't want to take their relationship any further. She'd say she'd been overwrought last night, which made her sound a bit of a wimp but was more or less true, and that it was unethical, as he was a client.

Of course he wasn't going to be a client for much longer; these past weeks had seen wonders accomplished in Raintree House. The study was more or less finished, its shelves and floor newly polished to a golden satin sheen, the paint crisp and matt on the woodwork. The only thing that Kieran had to decide on now was the style of the new balustrade for the staircase.

And when the house was finished they wouldn't need to see each other again. Although Kieran might want her she was certain he wasn't consumed by the fiery hunger that had changed her from the woman who had refused to let any man come close to her, to the one who last night had pleaded with him to stay. He didn't need to beg for his sexual release; there were plenty of women only too keen to give it to him.

The decision made, she leapt to her feet and began to work. It helped her bear the sick desolation that crept like a heavy, ominous tide through her.

Three o'clock loomed closer and closer. She caught up on housework, wrote a note to Wendy to thank her for the party, and did some more work on the make-over of the bedroom, hoping that she could provide the air of opulence her client so clearly wanted without making the room pretentious or affected. At two-thirty she showered, then donned a smart pair of navy trousers and a clear gold silk T-shirt, with a big cotton shirt over it patterned in darker shades of the same colours. She usually wore trousers when she worked; they made a decorator's life much easier.

Dead on three the doorbell rang. Sudden colour flamed through her skin as she opened it, but although Kieran's summer-hued gaze searched her face it was without a hint of the smoky sensuality she had come to expect from him. 'Have you heard the news?' he asked without preamble.

Her heart dropped. 'No.'

'Switch it on.'

She flew across to the radio. The announcer's voice flooded the room. 'A spokesman from the Ministry of External Relations and Trade said that the situation was being dealt with through officials from the Red

Crescent, the Muslim equivalent of the Red Cross. Diplomatic activity is intense, but as no one knows who is in power in El Amir it is impossible to say how effective it will be. The President of the United States and the Prime Minister of Great Britain have joined to condemn this latest——'

'Condemn what?' Tegan stared at Kieran, her eyes frightened. 'Kieran, what's happened?'

He didn't attempt to wrap it up in soothing platitudes. 'Word has come through that the hostages are to be ransomed for armaments. No guns, no releases.'

'And of course no government is going to sell guns to rebels,' she said numbly.

'No.'

She sat down, rubbing her forehead. Kieran came across and enclosed her in the warmth of his arms, holding her until the cold deadness in her thawed. 'Poor Blair,' she said quietly.

The telephone rang. She stared at it as though it were a snake and made no effort to pick it up. Kieran lifted the receiver and said, 'Yes?'

There was silence, until in a considerably altered voice he said, 'No, she doesn't want to talk to you,' and hung up.

'Who was it?' she asked dully.

'Rick Hannibal.'

'Oh. What did he want?'

'To ask whether you'd heard the news.'

'That was kind of him.' Looking down at her hands, she said, 'She could be there for years, couldn't she?'

'Possibly.' He hesitated, then said tonelessly, 'I'll see if I can find out what the hell's going on in there, but it doesn't sound good, I'm afraid. Come on, it's no use sitting around here; we've got an appointment in twenty minutes.'

'I have to ring Gerald first,' she said.

But Gerald wasn't home. Tegan put the receiver down and got up, trying to smile. 'Sorry. I'll just get my keys.'

'I'm not crouching in that sardine tin of yours all the way out to Titirangi,' he said instantly. 'We'll go in my car.'

The picture his objection evoked made her smile, but it was a pale echo of her usual radiance. 'OK.'

Kieran drove steadily through the afternoon traffic, mainly family cars taking the scenic drive along the ridge of the Waitakere Hills or heading for one of the western ironsand beaches. When they reached the outskirts of Titirangi she directed him into a narrow, almost hidden drive that ducked down a bush-covered hillside between two huge rimu trees.

Once there they wandered through a pin-neat workroom scented with the tangy balsam of timber, appraising samples of the cabinet-maker's skill and the work his two apprentices were doing. A tall, thin, silent old man, he was content to let them prowl while he sandpapered down a magnificent kauri sideboard that had, judging by its appearance, spent the last fifty years in a barn. They wandered around to the tune of whistled snatches of Twenties' airs and the smooth, sure movements of gnarled hands as they stroked the honey-coloured wood.

Tegan watched the sun sift down through flying golden motes, and thought dreamily that in spite of her fear for Blair, in spite of the fact that she was going to send Kieran away and it was going to hurt like nothing else in her life ever had, she had never been so happy. Just for this afternoon she was going to live in the present, not considering time or distance, or the bonds of friendship. She was going to savour every burnished, glowing moment.

That both she and Kieran chose the same balusters, graceful and slender yet with strength enough to inspire confidence, and the same smoothly rolled handrail, seemed to her to have the power of an omen, a sign of good luck for the future.

'You'll have to come and see the house before you start on it,' she told the cabinet-maker as they were going. 'The staircase is curved and suspended, so there could be a few technical problems.'

The old man's eyes gleamed. 'Ah, I like doing something with a bit of challenge in it. Where is this house?'

When Kieran told him he said immediately, 'I know it. My father worked there. I remember going to see it when I was a kid no higher than his knee. He was proud of that staircase.' Lost for a moment in his memories, he was silent, then thrust out his hand. 'I'll bring it back to glory for you,' he promised.

Back in the car, Tegan said softly, 'That's a nice coincidence. I think you must have been meant to have Raintree House.'

'I wouldn't have thought you were superstitious, Tegan.' Kieran sent a mocking glance her way. 'You said yourself that he's the last of the old-time craftsmen; with so much panelling in it, whoever bought the house would have ended up dealing with him. So it's not so much a coincidence as an inevitability.'

She pulled down the corners of her mouth. 'There speaks the pragmatic merchant banker.'

'You have something against merchant bankers?'

She gave him a slow, teasing smile. 'Come on—the Bible and all sorts of other books are full of the iniquities of usurers!'

'The only reason they didn't say something equally nasty about decorators is that until a few years ago there weren't any!'

'Rubbish. As long as there have been people who loved beauty there have been decorators. Oh, perhaps not as a profession, but the human hunger for beauty has been a part of our lives ever since our very distant ancestors strung the vertebrae of animals together to make a necklace, and put thumbprints, or used a stick, to make chevron marks on the pots they constructed.'

He smiled. 'All right,' he agreed amiably, 'your point is taken. You love your job, and you're damned good at it.'

It was a compliment all the more sweet for being so totally unexpected. Tegan hugged it to her like a delicious secret. 'Thank you,' she said in what she hoped was an assured manner.

His smile was a little lop-sided. 'I looked around Wendy and Nigel's house last night and realised that you designed them a place that fits them exactly. If you can do the same for me, that's all I can hope for.'

'Decorators Inc can do that small thing,' she said lightly. 'Where are we going?'

'Out to Piha. I feel like walking along a beach with nothing but the sound of the sea in my ears. All right?'

Tegan loved the wild west-coast beaches too. Smiling, she nodded.

Unfortunately the fine weather meant that Piha beach was dotted with people, too many for any sort of privacy. After parking the Jaguar, Kieran took her hand and they walked silently along the hard-packed sand.

Tegan felt the heat of his clasp right through to the nucleus of every cell in her body, and she winced, knowing that telling him she wasn't going to have an affair with him was going to be like ripping her heart out and throwing it to the wolves of despair.

But it had to be done. She didn't know that she could sufficiently overcome her fear of love to surrender herself so wholly. Her mother and father had a happy marriage, but the image that came to mind whenever Tegan thought of her mother was a seagull with a crippled wing; it could function, even look beautiful, but it could no longer soar with the currents of air high above the sea.

Admittedly, Kieran seemed to have a tolerant acceptance of her job, but he clearly didn't think it was particularly important, just as he hadn't thought his fiancée's job was. But Tegan had been telling the truth when she'd told him that her independence was precious to her. The idea of giving up even the slightest bit of it made her feel angry.

Kieran was pure dominant male, his attitudes honed by generations of autocratic men in his ancestry. He might pay lip service to the shibboleths of the twentieth century, but his instincts were those of a hunter, of a male who protected his woman with his great strength and the speed of his shrewd brain, and in return expected obedience. As Rick had said, he was a throwback to another, more barbarous age.

Gerald hadn't minded Blair's continuing to work, but Kieran considered Blair's husband a wimp.

The chill that had lurked behind the golden afternoon encompassed Tegan again. She turned her eyes to stare unseeing at the landscape, wondering what on earth could be done for Blair, whether she was at that moment suffering.

'Stop it,' he commanded astutely. 'Tearing yourself to shreds is not going to help her at all.'

'All right, you tell me how to stop.'

He looked down at her through his long, dark lashes, a smile barely curving his mouth. 'You've got guts enough to control yourself.'

His hand was warm about hers, somehow comforting. Of course he was right; she had to stay sensible and pragmatic, because falling to bits was going to help neither Blair nor the business they had worked so hard to build.

They walked on in silence while she tried to think of some way she could mobilise people and public opinion to get Blair out of the tiny country that had turned into a prison. But the thoughts in her brain chased themselves around and around, going nowhere, just adding to her apprehension.

She directed a sideways glance at Kieran. He should have looked too formal in his shoes and well-cut trousers on the beach, but he was a man who transcended conventions. The long breaking combers in the background, the thunder of spray and the pitiless reaches of the Tasman Sea behind him made a fitting backdrop to the stark purity of his profile, brutally outlined against the glinting, glittering sea. His mouth was compressed, as though he was considering some unpleasant course of action.

Her eyes lingered on the broad sweep of brow, the straight nose, the startling slash of cheekbone and jaw, and the surprisingly delicate moulding of lips which only served to emphasise the uncompromising strength of his other features.

Catching her by surprise, he turned to look at her. As though amused by her scrutiny, the corner of his mouth tucked in, and suddenly that disturbing sensuality blazed forth, potent as an enchanter's spell, untamed, lethal.

A group of people came towards them, their laughing conversation shattering the moment of silent communication.

'Let's go up into the sandhills,' he said. He bent and took off his shoes and socks, waiting while she slung her sandals over her shoulder. They made their way up the hot slopes with ease; clearly he exercised at least as much as she did. At the top she turned and looked away down the beach, trying to ready herself for the confrontation she sensed was coming.

'There's a bit of shade over there,' he said.

Nodding, she walked with him to where a scrubby teatree bush bent over a rock. He dropped his shoes to the ground.

Then he kissed her, and without protest, without even a pretence at resistance, she went under, lost in a conflagration of the senses that robbed her of the power to think, stole her intelligence and all her caution away until she was nothing but a collection of needs and blind hungers and an aching, savage urgency, her entire being aflame with passion.

That first kiss was hard and impatient, but Tegan revelled in the fierce demands of his mouth. However, almost immediately he eased the cruel pressure, and when he kissed her again it was different, surprisingly gentle, yet the claim was just as imperative. Tegan began to pull back; such tenderness was too appealing.

And she could not give in. He was too dangerous. Instinct warned Tegan that he would not be content with the compliant yielding of her body, the simple sating of passion. He wanted more from her, far more than it was safe for her to give. He wanted surrender.

His arms tightened, iron bonds about her. She could hear the heavy, slightly fast beat of his heart, and knew that she had done that—sent his pulses throbbing through him. It was too sweet, too hazardous; love was a cage, this pagan enchantment the warder. But when she lifted her weighted eyelids she was pierced to the heart, to the depths of her body, by the need burning in Kieran's eyes, and she gave him her mouth again, sinking back beneath the waves of desire he conjured from some unknown place within her.

'God,' he muttered against her lips. 'What the hell do you do to me? What is it about you that makes me forget everything, all the difficult, uncompromising lessons I've ever learned?'

The words drummed in Tegan's head, frightening her. When she tried to pull away he refused to allow it, exerting without any compunction the great strength she had always feared.

'You're hurting me,' she blurted.

'I'm not.'

He wasn't; he merely stood immovable as a rock and let her waste her energy by struggling.

A contradiction of emotions set her eyes glittering like tawny jewels. Anger warred with desire, outrage strove with a melting eagerness, and fear fought it out with a strange, atavistic need to trust.

Fear won. 'Please,' she said, her voice shaking hatefully on the word.

With leisurely confidence he kissed her cheek, the soft lines of her lashes, her straight nose and the fragile temple where her life-force beat like a small, betraying

kettledrum. Tegan held her breath, almost robbed of
volition by a paralysing flood of sweetness.

'You taste of summer,' he said harshly. 'Summer and
mystery, with your golden eyes and that warm, scented,
ivory skin, hair like black-crimson silk, and your proud,
patrician face, haughty and confident as a princess. You
walk through your world with such arrogance, such
thoroughbred, long-limbed poise, yet in spite of it you
yield to my touch so swiftly, so inevitably.'

Shaken by the deep satisfaction in his voice, Tegan
averted her head so that he could no longer see through
the transparent mask of her flesh to the emotions beneath. But she moved too quickly. Her mouth brushed
the place at the base of his throat where his pulse
throbbed. His big body froze.

For a timeless moment Tegan's heart stopped beating, until the instinct for survival broke through her
sensual trance.

No! She was going to tell him she didn't want an affair! She jerked her head back. Kieran's hands moved
swiftly, one imprisoning her against the quickening demand of his hips, one curling in the hair at the back of
her neck and with exquisite, slow cruelty compelling her
face forward until her lips rested once more on the tiny
pulse in the strong brown column of his neck.

With a shudder she opened her mouth against his
skin, delighting in the faint, potent scent that filled her
nostrils, the musky, masculine taste that filled her
mouth.

'Nothing to say?' There was a note in his voice she
couldn't decode, a sudden ragged catch.

'No.' The word came out as an indolent whisper. She
put out the tip of her tongue and with delicate know-
ingness licked across the thudding pulse. At that mo-

ment he was vulnerable, as entangled in the web of
passion as she was.

'I'm not surprised. What the hell can you say about
witchcraft?' The hand in her hair tightened, pulling her
head back to expose her face to him again. A quick, feral light blazed in his eyes.

He scrutinised the mindless pleasure in her expression, the soft, passionate heat of her trembling mouth.
Then he kissed her again, lingering with studied, sensuous experience, coaxing her mouth open beneath the
subtle insistence of his.

Tegan's bones deliquesced. Her hands clenched on to
his shoulders, and as he laughed low in his throat she
pulled herself into him, fitting against him with a recklessness born of the craving that clamoured through her
body.

He moved slightly, so that she felt him strong and
masculine and eager, and exultation coursed through
her like the stream of sparks from a bonfire at night.
She wanted him here, now; she wanted to lie down with
him and feel his magnificent force and power captured
and held by her, possessed and possessing, vanquish-
ing and vanquished, in that contest from which there
emerged no losers, only victors.

Primitive yearning surged through her in a tide as old
as time. *Now*, her instincts were calling, summoning,
imperative, *now*, with this man, *now, now, now*....

And then he stepped back, holding her away from
him with hands that trembled. 'No,' he said harshly,
thickly. He shook her. 'I seem to be always saying this,
but not here, Tegan, not now! Someone could come
down the sandhill any time.'

Slowly opening her eyes, she fixed them on him with
dazed incomprehension until the honeyed lassitude

faded. Although passion was still marked in the un-
yielding, arrogant contours of his face, he was once
more in control of it, as much master of himself as he
was of her responses.

Tegan winced as knowledge of her own complete and
utter lack of control ripped the iridescent fabric of her
desire. Shame heated her cheeks. He was supporting
her, his hands firm on her shoulders, scrutinising her
with a remoteness that chilled her through and through.
She tried to meet his eyes, miserably aware that she
failed. The faint stain of passion was still there in her
face, only waiting for a gesture to reactivate it.

Her mouth dried. She tried to pull away, but he
wouldn't free her, those aquamarine eyes seeing past her
puny efforts to the need and hunger beneath.

Of all men in the world to find this breathtaking ex-
hilaration with, Kieran Sinclair had to be about the
most dangerous!

'I'm sorry,' he said, his eyes searching her face. 'I
shouldn't have started this here.'

Fighting that perilous magnetism in every cell, she
called up her reserves of strength. 'I'm not thinking
straight,' she said huskily. 'Let me go, Kieran. Please.'

Refusal, obdurate, uncompromising, hardened his
glance. His hands tightened for a moment, then relaxed and fell by his sides. Instantly Tegan stepped
away, trying to put as much space between them as she
could.

'It won't work,' he said, the words measured and
unwavering. 'You can distance yourself, but it happened, and whatever it is that sets us both on fire, it's
not going to die.'

Uneasiness was a palpable force in her, dimming the sunlight. 'I don't want it,' she returned at last. 'I don't know how to deal with it.'

There was a return of that quick, untamed smile. 'No? You're lying to yourself. You want it, Tegan.'

'An affair.' The words were cold little pebbles in her mouth but she had to say them.

His gaze sharpened, stabbed through the barriers of control she was trying to restore, through the cool restraint. He said nothing.

'You're pushing too far, too fast,' she continued tonelessly. 'I told you I won't be manipulated, and I meant it.'

Not a muscle in his face altered, the angular lines remained the same, yet she sensed a change in him, a purposeful and deliberate watchfulness that drove shards of ice through her veins.

'I must have given you an extremely poor opinion of me,' he said crisply, 'if you honestly consider me the sort of man who would exploit you for my own advantage. An affair should be to the benefit of both parties. Otherwise it's seduction, and I don't indulge in that.'

Tegan hesitated, the claws of frustration still raking her viciously.

'Choose now,' he said, his voice cool and adamant. 'If you decide you're not interested, then I'll take you home.' And that will be an end to everything, his tone implied.

Torn, her emotions still seesawing, she gave cowardice free rein. 'I gather there's no place for me in your life as a friend?' she said, unaware of the wistful note in her voice.

His smile was jaded, so worldly that she almost cried out with the pain of it. 'I doubt very much whether we could stay friends,' he said. 'Come on, Tegan, you're not that naïve. When we kiss the earth starts careering off its path. Do you need a cast-iron guarantee where a romance is going? If it's promises you want, I can't give them to you. I don't believe in making vows I'm not sure I can carry out. But while you and I are lovers there'll be no other woman for me, and God help you if you let another man close to you. I don't share. Are you going to run away?'

'I should,' she said, lifting her chin a fraction.

He didn't pretend to misunderstand her. 'Make up your mind.'

'I'm trying to.' She wanted to say the words boldly, with a self-deprecating wryness, but they struggled to emerge from a mouth suddenly dry.

'What's the problem?'

Although her voice was almost a croak Tegan didn't dare moisten her lips. 'I don't know where I'm going.'

'And until now you've always seen your path ahead?'

Nodding, she pushed back a lock of red-black hair from her damp temple. 'Yes.'

'I'm not going to help you,' he said coolly, looking at her with heavy-lidded eyes. 'I don't want you to blame me for seducing you into acceptance. I want you, you know that, and you damned well want me. You may have persuaded other men to play your games, but not me, not this time. So what is it to be?'

He would do it. If she said she didn't want him, he would take her home and they would revert to being two professionals, client and decorator; there would be no satisfaction of the rush of desire that swept like a fountain of fire beneath her skin.

If she said no, she would always wonder what would have happened if she hadn't been such a coward. Not even to herself would she admit that she no longer had any choices in the matter.

'All right,' she said quietly.

But of course he didn't let her get away with that. With eyes that were mocking and speculative he scanned her lifted chin, her set mouth, the flakes of colour in her cheeks. 'Yes or no?'

He was trying to unnerve her. Well, two could play at that game. 'Yes or no to what?'

His smile was a mixture of challenge and provocation. 'Will you become my lover, Tegan Jones?'

'Yes,' she said, burning her bridges. Then, compelled by a self-serving desire to minimise the surrender she had once more made, she added, 'I won't move in with you, though.'

He lifted his brows but said quite pleasantly, 'I'm not going to ask you to. I like my privacy too.'

Tegan felt the most awful fool, but had to brazen it out. 'Well, that's all right,' she said, and stood wondering what one did next. Frustrated need still surged through her body, eating at what little composure she had left. The only consolation she had was that a nerve was jumping beside the hard line of Kieran's mouth, and the eyes that surveyed her were as dark and turbulent as tropical seas under a hurricane.

He was better able to hide it, but clearly he was as affected by those torrid moments as she.

'Let's go back,' he said, holding out his hand.

With racing pulses she put hers into it, and together they made their way down the sandhill and along the beach, not talking, content, Tegan thought dreamily, to be together. Her resolutions of the night before, her anguish over the radically opposed decision she had just made, seemed faint and far away now. Kieran blotted out all other considerations; her need to love him and be loved by him was too great to resist.

Dimly she knew that she was embarking on the most reckless action of her life, but what the hell? she thought. I've spent the last eight years being incredibly careful. I'm due for a wild, passionate affair, and if I get my heart broken—well, every woman needs to have it happen to her at least once.

'I'll drop you off at your place,' he told her. 'I have to spend the rest of the afternoon organising things. I'll pick you up round about seven, if that's all right, for dinner.'

'Would you like to have dinner at home?'

There was a momentary hesitation but his voice was easy and smooth as he said, 'If you want to, although I've reserved a table at the Lodge.'

The Lodge was a restaurant converted from an old gatekeeper's house halfway up one of Auckland's spectacular little volcanoes.

Hiding her disappointment, Tegan said, 'I'm not mad. Someone said the food there is the next best thing to ambrosia.'

He smiled. 'It's good, but I think that's overstating the case a bit.'

CHAPTER SEVEN

BUT it was delicious, just the same. It was a pity Tegan didn't taste much of it. Impatience rode her unbearably, made more intolerable because she had to restrain it. She had made her surrender out on the sandhill overlooking Piha; more than anything she wanted to taste the fruits of that decision, but she had too much self-respect to let anyone else in the magnificent room realise that the man who was eating his meal so—so *calmly* opposite her was the most important person in her life.

For him, it seemed, the evening was nothing out of the ordinary. Which of course it wasn't. He had slept with other women. She had never made love to a man.

Should she tell him? Was he expecting a woman of some experience, as befitted her twenty-eight years? Of course he was. But if she mentioned it he might ask why, and what would she say then? That she had never let another man get this far, that he was the only man to have made her feel like this?

If she told him the truth would he then decide that she was making too much of it? Humiliation crawled beneath her skin, followed bleakly by determination. She was not going to let her fears spoil things. He almost certainly didn't love her, but she loved him, and she wanted him. If their affair came to nothing, she would grieve, but it would be worth it. And making love was as natural and inevitable a part of loving as the day was of the night.

She lifted her head and gave him a glowing smile. His eyes narrowed into slits of pure saturated colour. 'What was that for?'

'I feel happy,' she said simply.

When he said, 'So do I,' she believed him.

So she smiled, and talked, although she couldn't recall what they said, and the food on her plate disappeared, although she couldn't remember its taste. Joy was a dazzle of feeling, needing nothing more than this man, this moment.

Afterwards they went out into the warm summer evening and drove through a fairy-tale city to the building in the heart of town where he lived on the topmost floor.

'You were a little unkind about your decorator,' she said as she glanced around. Excitement fizzled softly through her bloodstream, turning her eyes into glittering gold jewels.

'Do you like it?' His tone was tinged with distaste.

The beautiful, starkly modern room sitting-room was decorated in chrome and supple white leather, accented by a mirrored wall that doubled its size. An abstract picture like an explosion of gold and scarlet and a subtle, muted blue-grey, and two old, immense dragon trees provided the only colour.

'Yes, I do, very much. I'll bet Stan Forsythe did it. And I'll bet he didn't do it for you.'

He lifted his brows. 'No, he didn't, I'm leasing the place. Why?'

'Because he's far too good a decorator to put you in a room like this. You dislike it because it doesn't match your personality.'

'So you think you understand me well enough to create the perfect surroundings for me?' he asked almost
gently, and suddenly the air was charged with sensual
purpose.

Tegan's eyes dilated. 'I hope so,' she said, plucking
the words in a random fashion from her mind.

He came towards her, a humourless smile not soft-
ening his mouth. 'You're dressed very sedately tonight,' he said quietly, turning her around so that he
could undo the small button at the back of her embroi-
dered silk blouse. His hands were warm through the
fragile material. 'Positively demure; almost Victorian.'

He was standing so close that she could feel the heat
emanating from his big body, sensitising hers, making
her ready for his ultimate invasion of it. Tegan turned
her head, and saw their reflection in the mirrored wall.
Against his lithe, predator's elegance she looked almost frail, far outclassed in strength.

Her tongue dampened her lips. 'I didn't think the
Lodge was ready for me in my decorator persona.' She
tried to speak with some degree of composure, but her
voice sounded oddly creaky.

'They're used to anything there, but I must admit I
rather like the change. I prefer subtle pleasures. I know
that beneath this pretty thing there is skin like pale gold
satin, and that this skirt hides long, long legs, and a
waist so narrow my hands can almost span it. All for
me. I've always preferred searching for hidden treasure
to stumbling over it on the ground.'

His voice was deep and confident, the glinting aquamarine eyes holding hers in the mirror with hypnotis-
ing calculation as his fingers undid the next tiny button.
'And tonight you are a hidden treasure, an undiscov-
ered land.'

Somehow he had unfastened the shirt all the way down, and now with one skilful movement he unclipped her bra. Colour scorched through Tegan's ivory skin. His smile was a little lop-sided as he bent his head, and bit, very gently, at the base of her neck. At the same time his hands slid beneath the soft silk and cupped her breasts.

It was indecent to watch their images like this, yet she couldn't drag her eyes away, not when her blood began to run like wildfire, setting alight nerves she hadn't even known she possessed. Sensation streaked from the place where his teeth grazed her neck, from the lean strong hands that moved with slow purpose across her breasts; it pooled and gathered in the pit of her stomach, liquid, hot, irresistible.

He lifted his head and saw where her eyes were fixed, and he smiled. 'Now I know why some bedrooms have mirrored ceilings,' he drawled. 'There's something supremely decadent about watching yourself making love.'

His hands moved, pushed back the fragile material of her shirt and the bra so that they fell down her arms and on to the floor. The wide unstructured folds of the skirt band cinched her closely, contrasting with the slender pallor of her waist, the smooth, shadowed globes of her breasts with their tight nipples.

Then he turned her about to face him. 'But I find a mirror a poor substitute for the real thing,' he said huskily, his face setting into an expression of such devouring intensity that she gasped.

Shockingly, a hammering on the front door, impatient, threatening, tore through the weighted sensuality of the moment. For a moment Kieran's eyes remained fixed on her, then his lashes closed in sudden, quick

negation. 'Who the hell is that?' he demanded through
his teeth.

Tegan stooped, the river of desire within her suddenly chilling into ice. Clumsily she pulled on the bra
and set her lips together as she began to button up the
blouse. It needed only the top two buttons left undone
for her to be able to get into it.

'Turn around,' Kieran directed curtly.

This time she didn't look in the mirrored wall, and
there was none of the slow sensuous purpose with which
he had removed her clothes, just a quick deftness that
was typical.

She was tucking the blouse into her skirt when he left,
and was standing feeling, and no doubt looking, remarkably foolish when she recognised Andrea's voice,
high and uncontrolled. So Rick had been right, and it
was starting.

Kieran carried his sister into the room; by now she
was sobbing, her hands beating on his shoulders as she
tried to speak and couldn't, finally collapsing into wails.

Kieran sat her down on her feet. 'Look at me. *Look
at me*!'

'No,' she yelled frantically, struggling, but he was
inexorable.

His hand yanked her chin up; ridiculously childish,
Andrea squeezed her eyelids shut, but he must have seen
what he wanted to for he swore, a savage curse that
made Tegan wince and gaze at him with wide, shocked
eyes, eyes that dilated even further when he pushed his
sister away as though she contaminated him.

'I don't care,' Andrea shrieked, 'I don't care——'

Any further words were lost in the onslaught of another bout of tears. Quite suddenly she rocketed over

the edge into hysteria while Kieran watched her with flat, contemptuous eyes.

Tegan made for the other door in the room, found the kitchen and filled a glass with water. By the time she got back Kieran had deposited his sister on to the sofa and was endeavouring to make some sense of the words that tumbled like leaves in a high wind through the hiccuping and gasps.

'It's not that at all!' she shouted, just as Tegan came in. 'Where were you? I've been ringing and ringing and you weren't home, so I got a taxi and came over. Get me some brandy, K-Kieran, I *need* it!'

'Stop it!' Kieran's voice was austere with a concentrated, implacable authority. 'You know you can't have alcohol when you're like this. Drink some water.'

Andrea scrubbed at her exquisite face, blotched now by over-indulgence in unbridled emotions, and hiccuped again, before accepting the glass. Sobs still shook her slender form, and she was pale and sweating, but she managed to swallow a little of the water, and it seemed to calm her down.

Until she raised her eyes far enough to see who was standing beside her brother.

'You!' she shrieked, and launched herself at an unsuspecting Tegan, her hands crooked into claws, nails ready to rip and tear.

Instinctively Tegan countered with a quick chopping motion of one hand that sent the other woman reeling back, but although Andrea thumped heavily down on to the sofa she continued screaming like a banshee, foul words that made Tegan feel sick. Even when Kieran grabbed his sister and shook her so hard that her hair flopped over her eyes, she went on cursing Tegan with every epithet she could find in her far too extensive vocabulary. She looked demented, eyes wild, her face contorted, the gutter words spilling out until at last she grew hoarse, and then suddenly silent.

But Tegan wasn't watching her. She looked at Kieran, horrified at the unflagging patience with which he held his sister down, the stony indifference in every angle and plane in his face, the grim, hard opacity of his gaze.

When he must have been sure Andrea wasn't going to attack again he straightened, saying almost impersonally, 'I'll take you home.'

'Don't leave me,' Andrea croaked, her eyes burning in her pallid face. 'I don't want to go home. Rick's gone. He's not coming back. He said he wasn't going to, and he hasn't. Ask her where he is.'

For a split second Kieran's expression mirrored his shock. Tegan took a step towards him, but was brought up short by the instant reimposition of control so that she could see nothing in the sculpted lines of his face but an icy imperviousness.

'That's enough.' Kieran's voice was silky-soft, the danger in it all the more potent for being so quiet, so muted. He looked at his sister, his eyes unsparing shards of aquamarine. As though he'd given her an order Andrea launched herself once more at Tegan, who reacted entirely by instinct, bringing up her hand to slap the half-crazed woman across the face.

There was a terrible silence. Andrea's mouth hung open. The imprint on her cheek grew red, then faded.

Then Kieran put his arm around his sister's shoulders and said quietly, 'This isn't helping, Andrea. Calm down, and when you're feeling better I'll take you home.'

Andrea collapsed against him, and in a voice that was barely audible whispered, 'I'm sorry, Kieran, I'm sorry.

Don't make me go back. I don't want to go there ever again.'

'All right. You'd better apologise to Tegan.'

Andrea didn't move, but after a moment that muffled voice said, 'I'm sorry. I got overwrought, and I'm—I'm sorry.'

Thoroughly bewildered, Tegan gave the only response she could. 'It doesn't matter.'

Kieran picked up his sister, saying, 'Wait here,' over his shoulder as he carried her through the door that led to the rest of the apartment.

Suddenly limp, Tegan sat down in one of the white leather Wassily chairs. What on earth had Andrea been carrying on about? Clearly whatever she felt for Rick was infinitely more powerful than he believed to be so.

Noting absently that her hands were shaking in her lap, she wondered if someone had seen her having coffee with Rick that morning, and told Andrea. But no normal person would construct a whole scenario of betrayal for such a minor incident, which was what Andrea appeared to have done. Unless the person had problems.

With drugs?

At that moment the rumours stopped being rumours and assumed a much more sinister reality.

Kieran came into the room, his expression under rigorous control. Looking at him, Tegan couldn't believe that those moments in his arms had happened. Feeling betrayed, and more than slightly foolish, she asked tentatively, 'Is she all right?'

'Yes, but I won't be able to leave her for long. I've rung through for a taxi for you; put your jacket on and we'll go down to meet it.'

The lift delivered them too rapidly to the street entrance.

'I'll ring you tomorrow,' he said when the taxi drew up outside.

'Yes, all right.'

It was a cold parting, not redeemed by the kiss they exchanged, a kiss that seemed to her to be a mere politeness.

Once home Tegan tried to soothe her jangling nerves with a long, warm bath. It didn't work. She knew what was causing her tension—a rather painful cocktail of frustration and chagrin. She had been so happy, so filled with anticipation, and now she felt as though some slyly laughing god had taken his gift back.

Chilled by her abrupt dismissal, for that was what it had been, she forced herself to accept that for Kieran, naturally, Andrea's needs were paramount. It hurt, the pain only partly alleviated when he rang the next morning.

'How's Andrea now?' she asked tentatively.

'She'll survive. She's broken up with Rick, which is what all the drama last night was about. Did you listen to the news this morning?'

'Yes. It sounded quite hopeful, I thought.'

Yesterday's news item had been repudiated by the rebels who formed the *de facto* government of El Amir. According to one source the hostages were being prepared even now to be released.

'It does indeed,' he said. 'Tegan, I want to see you. Can I come around about eight tonight?'

She said carefully, 'I'm having an early dinner with a client, and then I planned to call in at Raintree House on my way home. Somehow the measurements for Mrs

Webber's curtains have been lost, so I'll have to do them again. My seamstress wants them tomorrow.'

'What time will you be there?'

'About nine, I suppose.'

'I don't want you alone in the house at that time of night. I'll meet you there.'

His concern made her feel warm and protected, a feeling she promptly squelched. 'All right. You can tell me what you think of the library. It's almost done.'

'Is it, indeed?'

'You did say you wanted it completed first.'

He said, 'I didn't realise it was so close to being ready. I'll see you then.' His voice altered, became deeper, a little more harsh. 'Andrea will never know how close she came to being thrown out last night, but I couldn't ignore her.'

'Of course you couldn't.'

'She relies on me,' he said abruptly, as though he didn't want to discuss his sister. 'Too much, but she's had a difficult life, and in many ways I'm the nearest thing to a father she's ever had.'

'Kieran, I understand.'

He said grimly, 'I could have murdered her when she turned up. The only consolation for me was that I had a very erotic dream when I finally got to bed. But dreams are no substitute for the real thing.'

She laughed. 'I know.'

'You too?'

Reassured by his admission, she said, 'Yes.'

'We're going to have to do something about it,' he promised. 'Even if we have to leave town to get away from importunate sisters.'

By the time she changed to go out to dinner with her client that evening the study was finished. And she was delighted with it.

The room glowed. Cartons of books had been arranged on the polished shelves. A magnificent Persian rug in the middle of the room was the perfect complement to a sofa covered in corded velvet of the same intense red as the rug. Tegan wandered around, touching the things she had assembled with such care: antique brass scales that gleamed on a kauri chest, blue and buff porcelain on the mantelpiece, a wicker basket of devil's ivy on an antique sofa table, and a flowering gardenia in an old blue jardinière.

It could have looked cottagy, but the proportions of the room, the glowing fabrics, and a certain formality in both the art that hung on the panelled walls and in the furniture placement gave it an air of sophisticated elegance. Just like the man who owned it all, the man she had created it for.

She was still delighted with it when she walked into it at nine o'clock that night and discovered that Kieran had organised coffee in an old silver coffee-pot, with a bottle of liqueur brandy and a small silver basket of mints on the low table in front of the sofa. Two brandy glasses, two coffee-cups and saucers, and a single gold rose in a silver vase completed his preparations. He had met her at the door and the kiss they had exchanged had set her pulses throbbing, but this evidence of his thoughtfulness made her throat tighten.

'When did you do all this?' she asked, excitement and tenderness vying for supremacy in her tone.

'When I got here a few minutes ago.'

She looked down at the jeans she had changed into, old and tight and washed so often they showed every line in her body. Over them was a shirt of clear navy. 'I didn't come dressed properly,' she said.

He looked her over thoroughly, clearly enjoying it, enjoying the colour that heated her skin, the smile that trembled a little on her mouth.

'You would make an old sail look like *haute couture*,' he said as he bent his head and kissed her.

The fervour of it eased some of the ache in her heart. Whatever had happened last night, it was quite clear that he still wanted her.

His lashes veiled the glinting streaks of fire in his eyes. 'Enough of that,' he said a little unsteadily. 'Sit down. Will you pour the coffee? Would you like some brandy?'

'Can it wait a moment? I have to have those measurements first thing tomorrow morning.'

He insisted on helping, so it only took a few minutes.

The tension was still there, but both were content to let it simmer for a while. The coffee was delicious, as was the liqueur. While the night settled around them they talked quietly. It would be like this, she thought with an uneven catch to her breathing, if they married.

'Where did all this furniture come from?' she asked, giving rise to the curiosity that had plagued her ever since she saw the lovely things. 'Are the pieces heirlooms, or did you collect them when you were in England?'

'It's family stuff.' For a moment the fleeting bitterness she had noted at the warehouse hardened his expression. He reached for her hand, pulling her over to sit beside him. 'You don't know much about me, do you? I'll fill in some gaps. My father's family are pastoralists; we own a high-country station in the mountains inland from Christchurch. My brother runs it now. My mother came from Christchurch. The men in her family were businessmen. My grandfather started the bank, and two uncles were running it, not very successfully, while I grew up.'

His arm was warm about her shoulders. Tegan relaxed, realising intuitively that in a way this was more important than a declaration of love—it was a declaration of trust from this intensely private man. Snuggled against him, she abandoned herself to the close mental communion which was just as sweet as the flash and flame of desire. There were so many aspects to loving Kieran.

'Moving from Christchurch to a back-country station must have been a shock to your mother's system,' she commented.

His laugh was surprised and mirthless. 'Yes. She couldn't take it for more than three years, and at least six months of that she spent waiting at her parents' house for me to be born. Finally she left to live permanently in Christchurch.'

Tegan nodded sympathetically. 'How terrible for them both. That's the worst sort of conflict, when one partner just can't live the other's life, because usually they're still in love.'

'I don't remember any conflict. Not then, anyway. We used to spend quite a bit of time up at the station, and eventually I acquired a younger brother, and then Andrea. The quarrels came later when my mother realised that the housekeeper on the station was my father's mistress, and that her son, a couple of years younger than me, was his son too.'

His voice was quite detached. Tegan looked up into a face carved from granite, his eyes bleak and cold as they looked down the tunnel of the years.

'Oh,' she said, feeling totally inadequate. This tangle, revealed so dispassionately, must have been harrowing for all those caught up in it. Especially the children. It was always worst for the children. But perhaps it explained why it was so important for him that his wife be prepared to give up her career for marriage. He might see that surrender as a sign of commitment, rather than a totally unfair imposition of his will on another.

His mouth curved in a travesty of a smile. 'Exactly,' he said obliquely. 'It ripped the family apart. My mother might not have wanted to live with my father, but she was a very possessive woman. She may even have loved him. If she did, it didn't last long in the light of those revelations. "Hell hath no fury like a woman scorned" describes her reaction perfectly.'

'I pity the poor housekeeper,' Tegan said angrily, repelled by his cynicism.

His laugh was low and unamused. 'I guessed that's how you'd react.'

'Did he love her?'

His shoulders moved in what might have been a shrug. 'Who knows? He never acknowledged Blade, my half-brother, although he left him quite a substantial legacy.'

'Do you keep in touch with him?'

'Yes.' He gave her an enigmatic look, then curled one of the red-black waves at her temple around his finger, speaking in a cool, unemotional voice. 'My mother was very bitter; she never forgave him for being born, and that bitterness rubbed off on to my brother and Andrea, but I could never hate Blade. He was as much a victim of the whole mess as we were. I went to his wedding a year ago. He's waited three years for Eden to grow up. She's a little thing, but she's got guts and character, and I think they'll be all right.'

His affection for Blade was clear in his voice. Suddenly overpowered with love for this man who was fair-minded enough to be able to empathise with a half-brother he had been encouraged to see as an interloper, Tegan kissed his cheek, and hugged him fiercely. After what seemed a moment of surprise, his arms tightened around her.

'It must have been a hellish situation for you all,' she said softly.

'Yes. Mother divorced my father. She was just as arrogant as he was, and she couldn't take the blow to her pride, especially as he made no attempt to get rid of Mrs Hammond. That was when I realised how important financial security was. My grandfather was as old-fashioned as his business; he had left my mother nothing, and her brothers were genteelly running the firm into the ground so they couldn't help much. My father paid for our schooling, but my mother had to pinch and scrape for years.'

Tegan nodded sympathetically. It was usually the woman who suffered most when a marriage broke up, especially financially.

'And Mrs Hammond had no security, either. My father didn't marry her, even after the divorce went through.'

'He sounds awful,' Tegan said, trying not to let her disgust show in her voice.

Kieran shrugged. 'Perhaps. He was the hardest man I've ever come across, but in the end I felt sorry for him. When Mrs Hammond died he had no one. Blade had

left, neither I nor the others would have anything to do
with him—he was quite alone. My mother was dead by
then, but she wouldn't have gone back to him. The furniture was hers.'

No wonder he surveyed it with that transient hostil-
ity. Lovely as it was, the furniture must be suffused with
hurtful memories of a bitter, desperate mother.

'And that,' he said determinedly, swinging his legs
along the sofa, taking her with him so that she was
sprawled on top of him, 'is enough about the far from
edifying lives of the Sinclairs. Tell me about yours.'

'There's not a lot to tell. I'm the only child of a
country doctor and his wife.'

'A much loved child.'

She nodded, her eyes lingering on the carved angles
and planes of his intent face, acutely aware of the hard
lines, the different masculine contours of his body beneath hers. 'Yes. How did you know?'

'It's a kind of sheen, a confidence that never dulls.
Happy children grow up to believe that the world is
good.'

'Were you happy as a child?'

He looked surprised but replied readily enough,
'Until my mother realised my father's unfaithfulness.
Then I hated him. In fact, it was only when I grew up
that I was able to see things from his point of view. Not
that I condone his behaviour, but he must have felt that
my mother had left him in all the ways that mattered.'

He slid his hand into her hair and pulled her face
down so that her mouth was only a fraction of an inch
above his. 'Kiss me,' he said softly.

She kissed the words from his mouth, kissed them
into oblivion, and when the kiss ended she knew that
this was the time, the occasion they had both waited for.

'You are so beautiful,' he said, freeing the buttons of her shirt and easing the material back so that he could unclip her bra. 'With your straight black brows and your skin like creamy ivory, and eyes as clear and glowing as topazes...'

He was no hasty lover. His lean hands shook as they moved over her skin, but there was nothing careless about their touch, or in the purposeful progress of his mouth as he kissed her breasts, tormenting her, driving her crazy until she began to whimper some unformed plea. Only then did his mouth reach the blossoming aureole in the centre, and an exaltation like no other pierced her, transfixing her on a point of rapture so keen that she gave a choked moan.

But Kieran was not satisfied with that; he found other sensitive places, some, like her navel, completely unsuspected by her, and explored them with his knowledgeable mouth and his skilled hands until her body quivered and ached with frustration, eager, palpitating, racked by hungry anticipation and a pleasure that grew sharper every second.

Hands clenched by her sides, Tegan bit her lips to keep the betraying little sounds back. He lifted her rigid fingers and placed them on his chest, spreading them over his heart. It pounded into her palm, out of control, shockingly erotic, and with no further protest Tegan traced across the damp, hot skin of his chest and shoulders, her fingers unbearably sensitive to the grain of his skin, the sleek, potent maleness of him. A blind, set smile curled her tender mouth as she discovered all that made him so different from her.

For months, it seemed, she had wanted to do this; her hands had been tingling with the need to know him, to make him hers through her fingertips, to absorb him through her senses. His slow, almost sedate courtship had banked the fires so that they burned more fiercely now he had slipped the leash of his control. Their mutual need was as obvious as the blatant desire she saw gleaming in his heavy-lidded eyes, narrowed and intent on one thing only.

He was so big... Yet Tegan was not afraid of his size, or the strength it implied. For he was as much at the mercy of this moment as she was. He groaned deeply as she traced the antique patterns of fine hair across his chest, the way his hair grew above his ears, the spot where his neck met his shoulder. She remembered how good it had felt when he had bitten her gently there, and she did the same to him, her anticipation rising as she felt his body tighten.

Emboldened, she found the small nubs between the scrolls of body hair, and nipped at them too, letting him feel the sharp serrations of her teeth, then delicately licked them, tasting salt and the faint, fresh flavour of aroused male. His skin was like oiled silk stretched over steel, his body held in such perilous stillness that instinct warned her he could not hold out for much longer

Unbidden, catching her entirely by surprise, her hips moved, pushing into him, begging for the only surcease, the only possible culmination.

She didn't even notice him slide her zip down, but she lifted herself automatically to free the passage of her jeans down past her thighs and knees. At last his eyes were able to see all of the taut pale flesh he had exposed, the small blue triangle of her pants. Tegan should have been embarrassed. Instead, her breath came quickly at the hunger lighting his eyes, the darkly intent desire that burned like aquamarine fire behind his astonishing lashes. An intense female pride shot through her; she lifted her hips to make his removal of the scrap of silk and lace easier.

'I know how Ulysses felt when he looked at Circe for the first time,' he said jerkily, resting his cheek against her flat stomach. 'Melusine, Calypso—you come from a long line of fairies, you Celtic witchwoman, inflaming your victims with the desire to see you gasp in pagan surrender. Yet your surrender is really victory. Your lovers have no chance...'

His hands slid down, probed, and he smiled, the feral, tight smile of a man almost at the end of his tether. 'Yes, you're ready,' he said, and, with a thrust that almost impaled her, linked them in the primal, ultimate embrace.

Tegan cried out, but welcomed him in, her stiff body loosening, enfolding, as she began to move in a rhythm as old as time, elemental, mindless, given over entirely to sensation and the primitive need to mate. Her surrender was as elemental as fire and wine; it was heaven and the sweet, pagan delights of earth; it was all that she had ever fantasised it could be.

Head thrown back, her eyes fixed on Kieran's starkly drawn face, Tegan gave everything she was, everything she could be, to the man who was now part of her. Yet it still wasn't enough. She felt a need, something more trying to free itself, and sobbed half under her breath with frustration.

'What is it?' He spoke indistinctly. 'What do you want? Tell me, and I'll do it. I'll give it to you. But you have to tell me...'

Drowning in the hot cobalt of his gaze, she couldn't respond. Her eyes drifted from the set, stark wildness of his face to the corded tendons in his neck. At first her mouth couldn't form the words; she gasped, 'I don't know—I want——'

She gasped again. Somewhere—some unattainable where—there was a destination that for all her striving she couldn't reach—until, caught in the grip of a force far stronger than anything she had ever experienced before, her body arced. A tiny cry tore through her as the slow waves started.

They came, erratically at first, then inexorably, pushing her higher and higher towards that glittering, distant peak, until at last she reached it, and was tossed beyond delight, beyond passion, into some realm of the senses where only sensation mattered, the brief, cataclysmic flowering of desire, of rapture. Almost immediately she was aware of the sudden clenching of his big body; the moment when he, too, reached that distant peak brought another rapturous implosion of delight.

Together they came down. Tegan lay cradled against him as the heated slickness of their bodies cooled and dried, and still neither of them moved except for the harsh rise and fall of their breathing. His face was pressed into the hollow of her shoulder; she shifted slightly and felt the gentle abrasion of his chin against her breast. Tomorrow, Tegan thought dreamily, she would be a little sore.

But oh, it had been worth it.

'I didn't intend to do this here,' he said at last.

She laughed softly. 'I'd have been very disappointed if we hadn't. We've had so many interruptions I began to wonder if we'd ever get this far.'

She felt his smile against her skin, but after a moment he sat up, pulling her with him. His arms tightened, iron bands around her; dreamily she listened to the heavy thudding of his heart, but then he put her

away very determinedly. 'I have to leave you,' he said.
'I'm heading overseas at midnight tonight.'

If he'd hit her Tegan couldn't have had a much
greater shock. Questions burnt her tongue, unspoken,
repressed. Making love might have moved her world
fundamentally off its axis, but it gave her no more rights
that she had had before.

'When will you be back?' she asked as she got quickly
into her clothes.

'I—don't know.' The hesitation was so slight that it
barely registered. 'I'll contact you when I get back.'

He followed her home, where he kissed her once more
with a drowning, hungry need that almost eased her
fears. Then he left her.

At ten the next morning a florist's van delivered
flowers to the office, exquisite gold and cream lilies
whose scent wove lazily around her in the soft air.

'Wow!' the receptionist said longingly. 'Aren't they
fabulous?'

'Lovely.' Tegan, who had spent a sleepless night,
wondered just what Kieran was trying to tell her. There
was nothing on the card except his initials. Had he
written it himself? She refused to pull out the contract
to check the signature, but halfway through the morning found herself doing just that. It warmed her heart
slightly to see that he had signed it, so he must have organised it himself, not just told his secretary to see to it.

It made her feel a little less like a mistress, and more
like a lover.

CHAPTER EIGHT

THAT night she went to bed early, pleasantly conscious of a number of aches and pains she had never experienced before. There were marks on her body, too, not dark enough to be bruises, but visible. Kieran had been a gentle lover, but at the end he had failed to temper his great strength to the delicacy of her skin. Tegan surveyed herself with what could only be called a smug smile before pulling on thin cotton pyjamas.

Surprisingly, because she thought she'd lie awake worrying about Blair, and missing Kieran, she dropped off to sleep almost immediately.

She was still in that first, deep slumber when finally the sounds of vigorous knocking at her door penetrated. Yawning, dazed, she pulled on a dressing-gown before stumbling out into the foyer to peer through the peep-hole. Andrea Sinclair stood outside, her brows drawn together in a frown.

Tegan didn't want to open the door. Her memories of the last time they met were altogether too vivid. But, driven by a hitherto unconscious fear that something might have happened to Kieran, she turned the key in the deadlock with shaking fingers.

'Hello,' she said in a strained voice.

Without acknowledgement Andrea swept in, looking around with something perilously close to a sneer.

'Yes, just as I imagined,' she said after a moment. 'It looks like a decorator's house.'

Tegan felt as though she'd been slapped in the face, but she curbed her first impulse to retaliate, and said instead, as mildly as she could, 'Perhaps that's because it *is* a decorator's house. As you clearly didn't come here to compliment me on my flat, what can I do for you?'

Colour high, Andrea turned on her. 'You can tell me where Rick is,' she said with open, deliberate arrogance.

Tegan's mouth dropped open. It took several seconds before she recovered enough to say feebly, 'I have absolutely no idea where he is. It's the middle of the night!'

'Are you sure?'

Still bewildered, Tegan returned, 'Yes, I'm quite sure. One thing I do know, however, is that he's not here.'

The angry note in her voice must have been convincing because after a narrow-eyed stare Andrea nodded. All arrogance drained away, she looked exhausted, as though her emotions were so intense that it was only by a ferocious effort of will that she could function. But when she spoke it was almost negligently. 'I just thought he might be.'

'Why?'

Andrea looked vaguely around. 'Oh, he's suffering from a crush, didn't you know? A crush on you. But I should have known he wouldn't be here. He knows which side his bread is buttered on, does Rick. And Kieran's possessive. So Rick backed off, but he's not stupid; he'll wait around until Kieran gives you the boot, and then he'll move in to pick up the pieces, just like a jackal after the lion's killed. I thought he might be silly enough to come around here asking for tea and sympathy, as he did the other day.'

'The other day?' Tegan knew she must sound like a total idiot, but something was niggling away at the back of her brain, and she couldn't concentrate on what Andrea was saying.

'Yes. Remember, you had lunch with him in Giorgio's.'

Kieran's sister seemed very calm, a far cry from the frantic, distraught woman of their last meeting. Tegan would have been relieved, except that she sensed Andrea's composure was not only artificial but precarious. Uneasily, not knowing how to handle this situation, still with something uncomfortably persistent tugging at her memory, she said, 'Oh, that. Yes, I'd forgotten.'

'Poor Rick.' Andrea gave a twisted smile. 'He thinks you're absolutely marvellous, and you don't even know he exists. Kieran does tend to have that effect on people, especially his women. Well, enjoy his attention while you've got it.' Her voice was ragged with remembered bitterness.

Tegan asked politely, 'What makes you think it's not going to last?'

Andrea stared at her. 'Experience. The Sinclair men don't have much staying power. It's not as though he's in love with you; Kieran doesn't fall in love. After all, how many men who look like Kieran and are as rich as he is are still single at his age? He was engaged once, but he dumped her quite mercilessly when he realised she wasn't going to be the sort of wife he wants. When he marries it will be to have children, and his wife will know what she can expect from him.'

'What are you trying to tell me?'

The thin shoulders moved in a slight shrug. 'Nothing you don't already know, if you're prepared to think about it. Kieran only took you out after Rick met you, didn't he? Oh, I'm not saying he doesn't want to go to bed with you—even for me Kieran wouldn't sleep with a woman he didn't want—but the only reason he took you out was to keep you away from Rick. And I'll bet he heated up your relationship after Patsy Berringer told him you and Rick were seen together at Giorgio's. I know she told him, because she told me she did. Even Patsy was scared by his reaction. He was totally furious. He'll always protect me. Sex is something Kieran has no difficulty getting—women have been throwing themselves at him ever since his voice broke—but my welfare is something else——'

'I don't believe you.' The words were torn, jagged and painful, from Tegan's throat.

'I'm sorry if it hurts.' Andrea's mouth trembled. 'Love does hurt, doesn't it, just as the song says? But Kieran's a lost cause, I'm afraid. Has he rung you up since he left?'

'No.' Only Tegan knew how reluctantly she said that word.

'Nothing's stopping him,' his sister said with a small, almost sympathetic smile. Something in her gaze, a kind of dissociated curiosity, pulled the little hairs on Tegan's skin upright. 'Are you all right?' Andrea asked suddenly.

Tegan swallowed. Her voice was harsh and thin. 'Yes, I'm all right.'

Hiding a yawn with her hand, Andrea nodded. 'If Rick does turn up, tell him not to bother coming back home. I don't want him any more.'

Tegan heard the door slam behind her before she realised that she was gone. Without thinking, she walked into the kitchen and made a cup of tea, every movement automatic as she went over what Andrea had said.

She drank the tea without tasting it while a slow, barely perceptible chill crept through her. Of course Andrea was wrong. She had to be; all talk of drugs aside, it was obvious that she was unstable. Her actions and behaviour had shown that. But, like the inexorable cooling of the year into winter, Tegan remembered that it was only after that second meeting at Raintree House that Kieran had suggested they bury the hatchet.

After she had been introduced to Rick.

Until that moment Kieran had been unremittingly hostile.

And it wasn't until he had come upon them talking on the terrace at Wendy Bannister's party that he had said he liked her, and wanted her.

Just before the scene at Piha Beach he had cut Rick off when he'd rung to offer his sympathy for Blair's plight. And he had known that she had been at Giorgio's with Rick that morning. Had that been why he had decided to take her to bed? Had he thought that if he slept with her Rick might go back to Andrea?

Tegan looked down at the empty cup, her face blank, the colour leached from her eyes to leave them a muddy brown.

Each incident was a damning nail in the coffin of the love she had discovered so short a time ago.

But she could not accept that Andrea had might have spoken the truth; her revulsions at the idea made Tegan shake her head passionately. No, it couldn't be so.

Without volition she got to her feet and began to pace the room, back and forth, back and forth, her long legs moving aimlessly. The pattern had to be sheer coincidence.

But even as she tried to convince herself the incriminating sequence of events danced in line, and she fell to counting them off, trying to persuade herself that she had got them in the wrong order. Painful indecision even drove her to check with the diary she kept, mainly for work, although each day she jotted down a few personal details as well. But there was no comfort for her there. In her own neat handwriting she discovered evidence that bore out Andrea's allegation.

Surely Kieran could not have instigated an affair just to keep his sister's romance viable? The thought made her physically ill. No, it was impossible to believe. He must know that the emotions were not so easily constrained. If Rick had fallen out of love with Andrea there was nothing Kieran could do to make him change his mind.

Insidiously, bits of information began to gather in her brain, all too easily forming a design. Perhaps all that Kieran hoped for was a temporary reprieve. If Andrea was addicted to some sort of drug, there was an excellent reason why she should not be saddled with the break-up of an affair. If, if, if...

'No,' Tegan said aloud, wincing at the sound of her constricted voice. 'This is all surmise.'

But it made a horrible kind of sense. She had, she thought grimly, allowed her own emotions to override the promptings of reason and logic. After all, Kieran had mistrusted her since the episode of Sam Hoskings. Why should he fall in love with a woman he considered to be no better than a whore?

Exhausted, she went back to bed, but there was no further sleep for her that night, and the next day she could only function by fuelling her energy with a mixture of sheer determination not to give in, and defiance.

She went to bed early with the headache that had been threatening all day now in full swing, and during the night she dreamed that Kieran was laughing at her.

When she awoke she lay cold and shivering. It was stupid to take so much notice of a dream, but somehow it seemed to bear out all her suspicions. Was her unconscious mind telling her that she had been living in a fool's paradise, deceiving herself as much as she had been deceived?

As the dawn broke through clouds to lay a soft, rosy patina over the city, Tegan decided she was not weakly going to accept Andrea's reading of the situation. When Kieran came back she would ask him outright. She would know, she thought, whether he lied or not.

But before he came back Gerald rang, his voice oddly distorted, as though, she thought with a catch of sudden, mindless panic, he had been weeping.

'It's Blair,' he said.

'What about her?' she said sharply.

'They've released all the other hostages, but Blair wasn't with them.' A long pause, then he said, 'They don't know why.'

Sheer horror froze Tegan's throat. After another taut silence she whispered, 'What do the people in the Ministry say?'

'They won't say anything.'

They talked for some time, she soothing, he slowly becoming less despairing. When at last Tegan hung up, she had only ten minutes of agitated worry before the telephone rang again. It was a journalist from one of the local newspapers, who wanted to know all about Blair. As she had on the other occasions when she'd been contacted, Tegan refused to say anything, but after she had answered the phone for the fourth time, the last two calls coming from international newspapers, she switched on the answerphone and tried to concentrate on work.

For once she didn't succeed. In the end she rang her mother and talked over the situation, drawing a measure of comfort from Marie's brisk practicality.

But that night, for the first time ever in her life, she took two aspirins in the hope that they would help her sleep.

Which could have been why she woke tired and heavy-headed the next morning. A couple of cups of coffee and a large, brilliantly coloured nectarine with her yoghurt helped a little, but it was with a weary heart that she went off to work. There Alana and the receptionist were eager for information, and for a while she listened to their queries and half-excited conclusions, until she could bear it no longer and shut herself in her office to work.

By the time she unlocked her front door late that evening Tegan was exhausted, her mind jumping from hideous visions of Blair in terrifying situations to the ever-present ache that was Kieran's absence.

She boiled an egg and forced it down, but the toast she made to go with it choked her. When the telephone rang again she almost ignored its summons, but the thought that Kieran might be the caller forced her to pick up the receiver.

It wasn't Kieran. Shattering disappointment deafened her to Gerald's first few words. ' . . . just rung up,' he shouted. 'She's in Singapore now, and she'll be home in twelve hours' time, at eight tomorrow morning.'

Tegan collapsed into a chair. 'Oh, thank God,' she whispered sincerely. 'Oh, Gerald, what wonderful, wonderful news!'

The night dragged, but towards morning Tegan fell asleep, and of course slept through her alarm, so she was running five minutes late when she got out to the airport. Gerald wasn't about, but as the jet from Singapore was delayed she decided he had probably rung up to check, been told it was going to land half an hour late, and sensibly allowed himself more time. Almost immediately, however, the sound of her name over the loudspeaker made her start, then sent her hurrying to the Air New Zealand counter.

Apparently the newspapers had found out about Blair's arrival, so to save her from any sort of ordeal by media the airline had set aside a room for her to meet her husband in. She wanted Tegan to wait there, too. From it they could be slipped out of a side-entrance.

Gerald was already there, talking jerkily to a couple of suited gentlemen who had Ministry of External Relations and Trade written all over them. They continued to stand around making desultory conversation until the door opened and in came Blair, thin and tired, her lovely face set in lines that spoke of rigid control imposed and held for far too long.

Smiling with relief, Tegan waited while Gerald flung his arms around his wife and kissed her. Blair swayed, and someone suggested a chair. There was a little bustle of activity, Gerald conferred with officials, and Blair smiled wearily at Tegan.

'Hi,' she said. 'Long time no see.'

'Blair.' Tegan hugged her ferociously. 'Oh, Blair, how are you, love?'

Blair's hug was equally fierce. 'I'm fine,' she said. 'At least, I will be when I—when I'm home.'

Tegan held her away, scanning her friend's face. Blair looked shadowy around the eyes, but that was probably fatigue, and if her lips trembled—well, Tegan's eyes were wet and she had to hold her mouth under strict subjection. 'It's wonderful to see you,' she said on a half-laugh.

'Believe me, it's wonderful to be back.' Blair flinched as Gerald tapped her on the shoulder.

'I'm sorry,' he said, looking wounded, 'but we have to go. There's a car waiting for us, and I believe someone from the Ministry wants to debrief you as soon as we get home.'

Blair nodded, her mane of copper and gold hair coming loose from the tight knot at the back of her head. 'Yes. Tegan, you'll come around soon, won't you?' She conjured up a weary smile. 'I want to know how things are going with the business.'

'All right.'

Two hours later Blair rang. 'How about coming around now?' she suggested, her deep, warm voice still strained. 'I've been debriefed, I know exactly what I can say to anyone, and I want to know how things are down at t'mill!'

'Things are fine at t'mill, you don't need to worry, but I know you will so I'll be there in ten minutes.'

Blair listened with her usual attention to Tegan's account of everything that had happened since her imprisonment. When her partner's voice died away she said on a long sigh that could have been relief, 'It

sounds as though you managed very well! I should have
known not to worry about it!'

'I was worried sick myself,' Tegan admitted. 'I didn't
realise how much I relied on you for the PR work, and
the flashes of inspiration that set me off on a completely new track.'

'We complement each other—me for the outra-
geous, you for the more conventional stuff. However,
you've obviously managed well enough without me!
What have you got there?'

'Various sketches and schemes for new commissions. A couple are already on contract, most are just
potentials. I thought you'd like to have a look.'

'Oh, I would indeed.' For the next twenty minutes
Blair flipped through the folders, occasionally muttering, several times scribbling a note.

Almost relaxed, Tegan sat back. The screw of tension that had been tightening within her since Blair's
captivity eased. It was good to have her back. Yet even
as she thought so she knew guiltily that only part of her
had been so worried about her partner. The other part
had been absorbed in her own affairs, in Kieran's place
in her life. It was not that she had worried any less
about Blair; it was just that Kieran had taken over her
heart.

Finally Blair put the folders down and stretched.
'Lord, but it's good to be home!'

Tegan said with great feeling, 'It's good to have you
back! Blair, how did you get out? One day we heard
that the person who held you was flatly refusing to give
you up, even after the other hostages were freed, and
then almost immediately you turned up in the Sultanate
next door! Did he change his mind?'

'No.' Blair's hand lay in a relaxed position on her lap. 'He didn't change his mind; he had it changed for him. I thought you knew all about it.'

'Me? How should I know?'

Blair smiled a little oddly. 'Because it was Kieran Sinclair who organised it. He came along for the ride, too.'

Tegan's mouth dropped open. 'Kieran did?'

'Yes. Apparently he's blood brother or something to a band of brigands in the next sheikhdom. He convinced them to sneak over the border, hold up the caravan that was taking me further into the mountains, and whip me away from under the nose of the pasha, or whatever he was.' Her teeth bit down hard on her lip. Then she shook her hair back from her face and went on, 'For a few horrible minutes I thought they were yet another faction in that faction-ridden little state. I didn't know whether I was being dragged out of the frying-pan into the fire, so I was a bit panicky. Fortunately Kieran muttered who he was in my ear, and we melted into the hills and back across the border. It was like something out of *The Sheikh*, but believe me, I have never been so profoundly grateful to hear a cultivated New Zealand accent before!'

'*Kieran* rescued you?' Tegan's eyes were still dazed.

'Yep. Rode up on an Arab stallion and carried me off over his saddle-bow. With a little help from his merry band of banditti. Which, by the way, is *strictly* confidential. No one is to know. Politics, of course. On the way home from the airport Gerald told me that you and Kieran have been setting the town on fire, so I concluded he got me out because he's in love with you?' she finished on an enquiring note, her eyes fixed on Tegan.

'No.' All the colour fled from Tegan's face. She sat as though she had been struck, trying to absorb the import of this. 'I didn't know anything about it. Oh, I knew he had contacts there, and he did tell me once that he had spent a few months with this band of bandits, but I never thought—he didn't even seem particularly interested.' She looked down at her hands, rigid in her lap.

'What's the matter?'

'He's not in love with me,' she admitted painfully, her mouth twisting as her eyes ached with unshed tears.

'Oh, Tegan.'

Tegan swallowed and blew her nose. 'It doesn't matter,' she said with a valiant attempt at briskness. 'I didn't come here to weep on your shoulder.'

'I don't know why not. It's a habit we formed when we were too young to know how bad it was—why try to break it now? What went wrong?'

'Nothing.' She gave a travesty of a smile. 'He just didn't fall in love with me. It happens. I have a horrible suspicion he thinks I'm a *femme fatale* of the worst sort, with a hungry eye for any available man. Including the one his sister was living with.'

'Why? Oh, that dates back to that wretched business with Sam Hoskings, I suppose. But if he thinks that, why did he ask you out?' Blair's face was beginning to assume what Tegan always thought of as her crusading expression.

'According to his sister, he saw her boyfriend making eyes at me and decided to seduce me just to keep Rick Hannibal for her.' Tegan tried to sound nonchalant, even slightly amused, but it didn't work.

'I don't believe it,' Blair stated trenchantly. 'Men don't act that way.'

'Oh, he *wants* me.' Tegan's mouth trembled, was firmed by an effort of will that showed.

'Tegan, Andrea Sinclair isn't very stable. She could have been lying, for reasons known only to herself.'

'I don't know what to believe,' Tegan confessed miserably, finding an odd sort of relief in talking it over. This was one of the things she had missed so much while Blair had been away. 'At first I thought just like you, but when I sat down and thought about it each major milestone in our progress towards bed was preceded by Rick Hannibal showing that he was mildly interested in me. Kieran is very protective of his sister; I've seen that for myself. And really, Blair, think about it. Why should Kieran Sinclair, who is probably the most exciting man in New Zealand at the moment, brilliant and powerful and well connected and fascinating, be interested in me? I'm not beautiful, he doesn't trust me an inch because of what happened with Sam, I haven't much to offer him.' She steadied her voice. 'I'm not even experienced. He could have any woman in the world; why would he choose me?'

'Believe me, experience isn't all it's cracked up to be,' Blair said. She sat without speaking for a moment, then said with crisp emphasis, 'Why *shouldn't* he fall in love with you? Plenty of other men have.'

'No, they only thought they did. They didn't really know me, so whatever they loved, if they loved at all, certainly wasn't me!' Ignoring Blair's snort of disbelief, she continued, 'The Sinclair men, so his sister told me, don't have a very good track record when it comes to women. I know his father ran a wife and a mistress for years, and Kieran was engaged once. Rick and Andrea both said he dumped her because she wouldn't give up her job to be a good little wife and mother.'

'Andrea said, Andrea said—it seems to me that Andrea Sinclair said too damned much! *If* it's true, you're well rid of him.' Blair's voice hardened. 'The rotten swine. The louse. The idiot! How dare he play with your life as though it's worth no more than a couple of copper cents?'

'When you're dealing with someone you're convinced makes a habit of collecting, then jilting men, it doesn't take much to dare.' Tegan had to be flippant, otherwise she'd burst into tears, and she was not going to do that. 'What's really amusing, in an ironic sort of way, is that Rick Hannibal's left Andrea anyway.'

'How do you know all this?'

'Oh, he told me first, over a cup of coffee at Giorgio's, and Andrea told me when she came to see me. That was when she also told me exactly why her big brother started an affair with me.'

Blair bit back an expletive, then leaned back in her chair, her lashes lowered as she considered. Tegan finished in a cracked, hasty voice, 'Which set me back a bit, as you can imagine, but I'll get over it. A man who could do that is not worth worrying about.'

'True.' Blair nodded vigorously. 'But as you don't *know* yet that it's the truth; why condemn him more or less out of hand? Why is Kieran so protective of his sister? Are the stories going around about Andrea Sinclair's addiction to tranquillisers true?'

'I don't know, but it would explain a lot,' Tegan said shortly. 'She's certainly not stable, whether it's drugs or just a fragile temperament.'

Blair's lashes drooped further. 'When did you last see Kieran?'

'Five days ago.'

'He flew to Singapore with me and handed me over to our people there. He couldn't have been kinder.'

Tegan went very still. 'He can be kind.' She hesitated, then went on, 'He's very protective, in a chivalrous way. That must be why he got you out—it was all right while you were with the other hostages, but when you were there all alone he called in his band of brigands. Why were you kept apart from the others, and left behind?'

'I happened to catch the eye of one of the rebel chiefs. No, it's all right; he wasn't able to persuade the others to give me to him until the day Kieran did his rescue, so I didn't lose my honour.' Blair silenced Tegan's horrified exclamation by saying, 'Haven't you seen Kieran since before Andrea dropped her bombshell?'

'No.'

'Then don't you think you should wait and let him give you his side of the story? It's so easy to be persuaded, especially when you're suffering from an inferiority complex, which is what you've got—heaven knows why. Really, this whole thing could be just the ramblings of a possessive, unstable, possibly addicted woman.'

'Don't you think I've told myself over and over again that it must be? But it makes a horrible sort of logic,' Tegan said wretchedly. 'In spite of everything, it hangs together. And after the Sam fiasco, he told me that he'd make me pay for it.'

'That was years ago!'

'Yes, I know, but even you, if you recall, thought he might still resent me enough to agree that I should keep out of sight when it came to Raintree House.'

Blair chewed her lip. 'It seems a little silly now. But yes, I did.'

'The point is, he was still furious with me at first. He behaved like a pig until—until Rick Hannibal arrived on the scene. And then he changed.'

'Oh, it all sounds too melodramatic for words. Listen, just don't do anything silly, like burning your boats, all right?' Blair looked up as Gerald came in.

'You should have finished talking business by now,' he said cheerfully. 'I've made a cup of tea for us all, and then, Tegan, I think you'd better get home, because poor old Blair is just about falling asleep.'

Not for the first time Tegan wondered why Blair had married Gerald. He was a dear, but he was so—conventional was probably the word she wanted, whereas Blair was warm and clever and far from staid. Still, it was a happy marriage, so perhaps they complemented each other.

Kieran rang her the next morning as she was putting the kettle on for her first cup of coffee. Hiding the dizzying mixture of soaring expectancy and leaden fear, she said in as level as voice as she could manage, 'When did you get back?'

'About four hours ago. Work's piled up here so I'll be stuck all day, but I'd like to see you tonight.'

'Come and have dinner with me here.' Her unfolding delight was marred by a thin thread of foreboding, but she refused to let it show.

She could hear his smile in his voice. 'I'd like that. I'll see you about seven, shall I?'

She spent the rest of the day buying for, then preparing, the most wonderful meal she could create. A sudden windshift to the south in the afternoon brought with it rain and a quick, autumnal chill to the air. Tegan turned on the heating before dressing very carefully in indigo trousers and an apricot waistcoat, with a large,

loose, paprika chiffon shirt over it, clipping her trademark huge earrings on, these ones with a look of the
Orient. Casually smart, she decided, but not sexy. She
would make him realise she was not just some toy to be
used whenever he felt like it, to be thought of with mild
contempt.

Later, she knew, if Andrea was right, grief and pain
would rip her poise to shreds, but not until after he had
gone and his sordid little plot had been exposed to the
full blast of her scorn.

But—oh, she had to trust that the whole thing was
just the result of a series of coincidences and Andrea's
febrile mind!

On time as always, he rang the doorbell as her clock
began to chime seven. Incurably punctual herself, Tegan
thought savagely that it probably showed a mind set
tightly in grooves of rigidity—a mind that held old-
fashioned ideas like revenge, and protecting one's sister, firmly to the forefront.

Kieran made no attempt to kiss her, and the sea-
coloured eyes were opaque and enigmatic as he came
through her door. Tegan's chin lifted fractionally.

First things first. 'Thank you for your help in getting Blair out of El Amir,' she said, trying to sound
normal and managing only a certain wintry calm.

'You weren't supposed to know anything about that.'
His voice was measured, but the anger he couldn't quite
hide hardened it.

'I won't be telling anyone else, I promise you. I presume it might jeopardise your business if it became
generally known that you had helped her get free.'

His brows lifted. 'Quite possibly.'

Why didn't he say something? He was, she thought,
that flame of anger burning deeply inside, going to

make her do all the work, even though it was clear he realised she was furious with him. Or did he think she was so besotted by the technical expertise of his love-making that she would continue the relationship, in spite of understanding he had only used her for his own purposes? Ruthlessly she tamped her emotions down; when she was upset she was vulnerable.

Cool, calm and emotionless—that was the way to deal with this situation.

'I had a fascinating conversation with your sister a couple of days ago,' she said evenly.

His eyes narrowed. She thought they faced each other like two antagonists of some distant time, woman and man locked in a primeval battle. At least it wasn't likely to turn physical.

'Did you?'

'She told me you decided to take me out because Rick started to show that he liked me.'

His expression didn't alter. 'And what,' he drawled after a taut moment, 'was your reaction to that?'

At the memory of that anguished, horrified search through her memory, the days since when she had tee-tered from the conviction that he was false to an insistence that he must feel something for her, Tegan's face grew grim. But she pushed the words out. 'I realised that she had a point. You have to admit that you showed no interest in me until he turned up at the house with you.'

'I see.'

And that, apparently, was where he was going to leave it. He was already turning, showing her that she was nothing to him, that he had no further use for her. Common sense told her to keep quiet, to let it end like that, but the words came tumbling from her lips. 'Was she right?'

'You believed her.'

'No!'

But he lifted his brows, the blue-green eyes hard and unemotional. 'Yes. You want me to convince you that it's not true, so you believe her. Yes, she was right.' He watched her paling face with cold dispassion. 'I knew right from the start that you were nothing but an opportunist, and if Sam Hoskings hadn't convinced me, then overhearing you turn down Peter Whatever-his-name-is at the Pipers' party would have. I cringed for the poor bastard when he promised you everything, and you threw it in his face, without even the decency to sound sorry about it. I decided then that you needed to be taught a lesson, but it wasn't until Rick started sniffing that I knew I was the logical choice to do it.'

She should be in agony, Tegan thought with a strange detachment, but apart from a lump of lead in her chest where her heart normally was she felt nothing but cold. Even her voice was remote, light, a little ironic. 'How easy I made it for you! I fell into your hand like a ripe plum.'

'A ripe peach,' he said, measuring her with a look as insulting as it was prolonged. 'Or a long-stemmed rose, in shades of ivory and gold and a red so dark it's almost black, just ready to pick.'

Colour drained from her face. 'Well, you've had your revenge,' she said, still in the same unemotional tone. 'You've paid me back for Sam. Now go.'

He smiled and pushed the door closed behind him, snapping the deadlock into place. 'Not so fast,' he said softly, silkily, holding her rapidly dilating eyes with his own. 'By your system of reckoning, you owe me for getting your friend out of El Amir, for putting a variety of commissions your way, for letting you do my house—I'd say you owe me a hell of a lot.' Without taking his eyes off her he began to unbuckle his belt. 'And you can repay me flat on your back.'

Shock held her transfixed until he flipped the buttons of his shirt open. Then she croaked, 'Don't you dare!'

'I don't need to dare; there's nothing I need fear from taking you to bed,' he said, slinging his jacket and shirt over the console table. 'We've already done it, or had you forgotten that?'

No, she hadn't forgotten. Every moment of those hours was engraved on to her memory. His gaze had fastened on to her mouth and he seemed unable to look away. Tegan knew what he was feeling, for she was feeling it too—the inexorable, remorseless leap of passion, firing her bloodstream, shaking her mouth, sending off enough signals to light a winter sky.

She tried to kill it, tried to cover up by saying harshly, 'I won't let you rape me,' as she averted her eyes from his golden-brown torso with its oddly formalised pattern of hair across the smooth skin.

He came towards her, big, so big that real fear weakened her bones, kicked her in the stomach. How many times had she wondered what it would be like to see him slip the leash of his will? Her fearful eyes ranged his face, but she couldn't see any loss of control there—nothing but a hard purpose that sent her backing away.

'Why should I draw the line at rape?' he drawled. 'A man who deliberately set out to seduce a woman to keep her away from his sister's lover has already committed rape of a sort, wouldn't you say?'

His hands caught her by the shoulders; seconds later her fragile shirt was fluttering to the ground, and she stood before him in the indigo trousers and the sleeveless little waistcoat.

'Surprisingly sexy,' he said deeply, and pulled her towards him.

'No, don't—*don't*—' Galvanised into struggling in earnest, she turned her face away, but he laughed and bent his head to the spot where her neck joined her shoulders. Only he didn't kiss; he bit, not very gently, and she cursed the sudden singing in her blood, the quicksilver response in every one of her cells.

'Kieran, are you telling me that you didn't—that Andrea was wrong?' she gasped.

'No,' he said coolly, running his hand down her back and under the waistband of the indigo trousers.

Sensations savaged Tegan with a potent, violent intensity. She dragged in her breath and both hands flew to haul his intrusive fingers away. As though this was what he had been waiting for, he caught her wrists together behind her back and pulled them down, so that her breasts jutted out, brushing against the wall of his chest.

'I'm not telling you that at all,' he said now, watching with insolent appreciation the quick rise and fall of her breasts beneath the apricot waistcoat. 'I've already told you that Andrea was right; I had no intention of having anything to do with you until I saw how Rick was looking at you. Then I decided that you had to be neutralised, and as he has a healthy respect for me the best way to do it was to claim you for my own. Which I did.'

'You bastard!'

He didn't even have to use his great strength. He let her waste hers trying to break free, all the while slowly forcing her closer until she was pressed against him. He was, she realised with horror and a sick excitement, aroused, just as she was.

What sort of a woman was she, to want a man who had used her so ruthlessly?

'We're well matched, then,' he taunted, lowering his head. 'Because you may have forgotten that you almost drove Sam Hoskings to suicide, but I haven't.'

She had no chance to object. His mouth crushed hers in a kiss as demanding, as wild and consuming, as the ocean. Ruthlessly, holding her wrists in a grip that didn't hurt but permitted no movement, he forced her mouth open, his free hand pressed between her shoulder-blade so that she had nowhere to go, no chance of escape.

The heat of his body scorched through the material of her clothes, setting fire to her treacherous instincts.

When the kiss was over she said brokenly, 'Please don't. I can't give you whatever you came here for——'

'Oh, this is what I came for—a moment's forgetfulness, the physical surcease that for a while at least sates the hunger gnawing at both pride and honour. You can give me that, Tegan. After all, you owe me.' The words sounded like an obscenity.

He was white about the mouth, and her eyes widened at the tell-tale sheen of moisture on his temples, the dilation of his eyes until the dark pupil swallowed up all but a thin rim of colour, intensifying it into a blaze like the corona around the sun in an eclipse.

'No,' she whispered, appalled.

'Yes. I wonder how long it will take for me to get sick of sex that's mere payment?'

Tegan had never before experienced anything like this sinister amalgam of pain and pleasure, for barely repressed desire came surging up through the anguish and the bitter betrayal, through the anger and the despair.

All restraint burnt away, he kissed her as though he was dying for her, as though she was everything to him, as though he had starved for her down untold aeons; and she responded, demanding everything, holding back nothing.

Outside rain beat down, but here in this room it was warm and dry, and the lamps gilded the ivory of Tegan's skin, lit to bronze the smooth flexion of muscles as Kieran lifted her and put her on the sofa. For a moment common sense attempted to break through the rage of desire that held her in thrall, but he came down beside her and his head bent to her breast, and she shuddered and said his name in a high, wild voice, lost once more in the treacherous jungles of passion and carnality.

He made love to her with such animal intensity that she couldn't speak. Kieran's touch, the subtle ferocity of their lovemaking, the rapturous, molten response he coaxed from her body—all these banished everything but need from her brain.

This was what Tegan had wanted since she had looked at him the first time and without realising it her body had called to its other half. That subliminal call had been the song of the siren, pagan, perilous, reckless almost to madness, but it had another aspect—this ecstasy, where the world narrowed down to a firelit room and this man, and an untamed, exultant subjugation.

Then Kieran pulled away with an oath that drove the smoky fulfilment from her eyes with an instantaneous recognition of just what she had done, how close she had come to begging him to take her, to giving him a surrender that would haunt her for the rest of her life.

'As it happens,' he said through his teeth, picking up her shirt to throw over her, 'in spite of your charming enthusiasm I don't want to go to bed with a woman who thinks I'm no better than a rapist.'

Nausea gripped Tegan in its clammy clutch. Pressing a hand to her midriff, she carefully sat up, keeping her face averted. Her plans for making him understand, for forcing him to accept that he had been wrong in his judgement of her, were shattered.

If he could make love so—so fiercely, yet so tenderly, and still feel nothing but disgust for her, then she had no chance of convincing him. Tegan didn't even know that she wanted to. Betrayal was acrid on her tongue, etched across her heart. The only thing she could take with her now was pride.

'Please go,' she replied tonelessly, huddling into her shirt.

CHAPTER NINE

SLOW weeks dragged by, the tail-end of summer merging imperceptibly into autumn although the heat and the humidity stayed, made worse when rain drifted in from the north and enveloped the city like a warm, wet duvet.

Tegan discovered that hell could be as much a part of life as joy. She supposed she functioned in a more or less normal fashion; certainly she went to work, and produced schemes, and signed contracts. Kieran had been right. As soon as people saw what had been done at Raintree House, Decorators Inc was flooded with enquiries, many of which looked likely to turn into definite contracts. No one seemed to notice anything different about her. Blair looked hard at her once or twice, but to Tegan's relief made no comment.

Oh, when would she lose this ever-present ache in her heart, this feeling of emptiness, of incompletion? She even found herself hoping that the contraception he had used had failed, until her body informed her unmistakably that there would be no child. Common sense told her she was mad, but deeper, more fundamental yearnings tore at her heart.

She missed him so much. She missed his stimulating conversation, the way they sparked off each other's minds. And his presence, the formidable physical force that was Kieran Sinclair, his smoky, dangerous charm, the sheer tactile pleasure of skin and hair and the blazing brilliance of his eyes, the sculpture of high cheekbones and straight nose and sensual, determined mouth, the arrogant jut of his jaw.

But after several weeks she realised she had to accept that it was over, and strive to attain some sort of peace to take the place of the turbulent grief and bitter rasp of betrayal. The only way to accomplish that was to stop mourning and start living again, to act as normally as possible.

It was a decision she carried out immediately, taking herself off to an exhibition at one of the fashionable galleries. A client wanted something from this particular artist to fill an empty space on a wall. Tegan had tried to persuade the woman to choose for herself, but she refused. The artist was newly fashionable and she wasn't sure enough of her own taste to know which one she liked the most.

Or even, Tegan thought wearily, whether she liked his work at all. Tegan didn't. However, she plodded stolidly around the gallery. She had almost got back to the door and was looking forward to a cup of coffee when a man bumped into her from behind.

'Sorry,' he said automatically.

Startled, she looked over her shoulder.

'Oh, hello,' Rick Hannibal said without enthusiasm. 'What are you doing here?'

'The same as you, I imagine. Looking.'

'What do you think of it?'

'It's interesting.' Stupid words, banal reactions, but they helped fill the silence. Tegan had become an expert in filling up empty spaces.

'Bloody pretentious, if you ask me. Come and have some lunch,' he invited edgily. 'You look as though you could do with something to eat.'

Scotching her first impulse to refuse, she agreed because, she admitted silently and scathingly, she wanted to hear something, however small and unimportant, of Kieran.

Once seated with a salad in front of her, she asked, 'Are you and Andrea still apart?'

He grimaced. 'Yes.' After a moment he looked up at her. 'I gather she came to see you.'

'She said she thought you might have been there, although she must have known you wouldn't be.'

After muttering something succinct under his breath he said, 'I'm sorry. She had no right to get you embroiled in our affairs.'

'She seemed to think I was already embroiled in them.' Tegan was unable to prevent a note of bitterness in her voice.

Rick said curtly, 'As I told you, she's always been possessive—of her brothers, of her mother, of me. I think it goes back to what happened in their childhood—do you know——?

'Yes, Kieran told me.'

'Did he now?' His brows shot up. He directed a long, considering look at her before continuing, 'You're honoured. According to Andrea he never talks about it. It affected them all, but Andrea especially. Think how it would be to have your happy life suddenly shattered, to be told by your mother that your father no longer loved you—which she did, the stupid b—woman. It's no wonder Andrea feels she has to cling desperately to everything she loves in case it gets torn away from her.'

Tegan said slowly, 'You really do love her.'

'Surprised? Well, yes, I suppose you are, after I handed you all that guff about leaving for England. I was still furious with her then. Of course I love her. I wish to God I didn't.' He surveyed his omelette with an unseeing eye, then looked challengingly at Tegan. 'I suppose you've heard she was addicted to tranquillisers.'

'I'd heard rumours,' she admitted.

He shrugged. 'There are always rumours. This one was true. She behaved pretty outrageously for a while when Kieran was overseas. He straightened her out when he came back, and she's all right now. Well, almost all right. But although she's been clean for a year she's still not a hundred per cent, and she hasn't been getting any better.' He put down his fork and stirred his coffee absent-mindedly. 'I would have gone back when Kieran was called away, but her doctor decided that she could cope.'

Tegan said blankly, 'I'm sorry, I don't understand.'

He shrugged. 'When I'd cooled down after the fight I rang Kieran. He said this time he couldn't stick around, he had to go overseas, so we went to see her doctor. She's still in therapy. The great man hummed and hawed, but finally admitted that possibly this was the trigger she needed to get her off that plateau. Kieran's always been there for her, but this time she'd have to deal with it alone. So I stayed away.'

His tone revealed how difficult it had been. Tegan asked, 'And how is she now?'

'So far, so good. Now all we have to do is wait for her to tell me she wants me back.' Deep, jagged emotions lurked behind his smile. 'That's if she does want me back, of course. But she'd done well. Kieran's been overseas for the last six weeks, so this time she's had to manage by herself, and her therapist's pleased with the way she's coped.'

What little appetite she had completely gone, Tegan looked down at her salad. So Kieran hadn't even been in New Zealand.

Determination hardened Rick's features as he went on, 'I want her to ask me back because she loves me, not because she needs a man to lean on. She has to accept that we've only got a future if she gives up running to Kieran every time something goes wrong in her life.'

The coffee was hot and dark, delicious. As she put the cup down, Tegan said what had been racing around her brain since he'd divulged what had happened. 'So Kieran knows all this?'

'Yes, of course he does.'

'Then, if——' She fell silent. If Kieran knew what had happened, then he must know that Rick had no intention of leaving Andrea permanently. Which meant that he . . .

Her lips began to tremble. She took another large sip of coffee and wished she was alone. If what Rick was saying was correct—and he looked patently, obviously truthful—then there had been absolutely no reason for Kieran to pretend to be attracted to her.

So Andrea had been wrong.

And, misled by her own particular devils of insecurity and suspicion, Tegan had made the biggest mistake in her life when she had accused Kieran of using her.

'What's the matter?' Rick asked.

Tegan looked at him with eyes gone muddy and opaque. 'I—nothing.'

'Feel free to dump on me,' he said drily. 'Fair's fair.'

'Have you seen Kieran lately?'

He nodded, sending her a look from beneath his lashes. 'He made a flying visit home a week ago. He's gone all grim and silent; everyone took to ducking for cover whenever he came into a room. He told a cabinet minister he needn't come back to him for advice until he understood how the money market worked. And although Kieran, being Kieran, got away with it, you just don't go round saying that sort of thing to cabinet ministers!'

'Perhaps something's gone wrong with his affairs,' Tegan said quickly.

Rick's brows lifted. 'Not the business,' he said. He gave a wry smile. 'You don't want to eat any of that, do you? Neither do I. Let's go. Can I give you a ride anywhere?'

'No, I've got my car,' she said automatically.

Outside, Tegan blinked at the sunny street, feeling as though she'd been in the gallery for hours.

'I'll see you around,' Rick said casually. 'Soon, I hope.'

'Goodbye.'

Back home Tegan wandered through the empty rooms before forcing herself to sit down and try to work. But after a few desultory strokes she put down her pencil and sat for a long time with her hands clasped loosely in front of her, wondering what she should do.

The fact that both she and Andrea had been so wrong about Kieran's motives didn't necessarily change anything. He still saw her as the woman who had driven

Sam Hoskings to disaster. That last, contemptuous evening had shown her just how little he thought of her. Her soft mouth trembled. Putting her head down on her arms, she wept. Then she washed her face and rang home.

'I thought I might come and see you this weekend,' she told her mother.

'Darling, we'd love that!' Marie's voice was warm and happy, excited at the thought of seeing her.

It was a peaceful weekend. Of course her parents knew something was wrong, but they didn't pry. Safe in their undemanding companionship, Tegan smiled and talked and pretended a serenity she didn't feel. She spent hours walking along the beach, a sweep of sand protected from the worst the sea could offer by the cluster of Mercury Islands dotting the horizon. Slowly she managed to reach some sort of tranquillity.

On Sunday afternoon when her father was fishing with a friend she and her mother sat beneath the climbing rose that rioted over the pergola and looked out across a sea the colour of Kieran's eyes. Sniffing inelegantly, Tegan scrabbled for a handkerchief to scrub the sudden hot tears away.

'Have a tissue,' her mother said, handing her a box. She waited until Tegan had mopped up before asking, 'Do you want to talk about it?'

'Not particularly.' Tegan softened her refusal with a lop-sided smile. 'I'm just crossed in love. Mum, do you ever regret giving up your career for life here with Dad?'

Surprised, Marie hesitated, her black brows drawn together. 'I could say no,' she said thoughtfully, 'that loving him made it easy, but it wouldn't be entirely true. Sometimes I've wondered what my life would have been like if I'd gone to England. But—life is a matter of compromises. Young as I was, I realised that I couldn't have it all. Actors rarely have settled, happy marriages, and actresses especially find it difficult to be the sort of mothers they'd want to be. I loved your father and wanted his children.'

'But if it was a vocation...'

'I would have made a good actress, but whether I had the ruthlessness I'd have needed to get to the top—I don't know. I suspect not.'

'Dad could have gone to England with you while you found out.'

'Yes, but there was no doctor here. They needed him. I understood that. Anyway, when I decided to marry him I promised myself I wasn't ever going to yearn for a future that might or might not have happened. I was lucky to be given such choices; most people in this world have to take what they can get. And I'm very happy here. Your father and I have a marriage that works, I love living in the most beautiful place in the world, and I lead a satisfying life.'

'I used to think that Dad had no right to force you to make that choice.'

'He didn't force me.' Marie smiled in reminiscence. 'He left me, told me that he didn't ever want to see me again, that it was over. He wanted me to have my chance. I thought about it long and seriously, and then I seduced him very thoroughly, because I knew he'd come over all honourable and insist we marry. Which he did. Just as well, actually. You were conceived then.'

Tegan couldn't stop the shock that showed in her face. Not without satisfaction, her mother laughed gently. 'You have to choose the way you want to go, then grab your opportunities,' she said, 'and make the most of them, without any regrets for the ones you didn't take. Otherwise you'll probably never be happy, always looking over your shoulder at what might have happened instead of enjoying what did.'

It would have been easy to confide in her, but Tegan couldn't bring herself to do it yet. She nodded, and began to talk about her latest commission.

Her father arrived back with a large gurnard and a story of the massive snapper that got away. As she left them to change for dinner, Tegan intercepted the smile her parents exchanged—warm, amused, infinitely loving. Something tight unwound in her heart. Compared to Kieran and Andrea's childhood, hers had been paradise.

They were just about to start the meal when a car swung in off the road and along the drive. Marie got up to look through the window.

'Damn,' Rhys Jones said, but with resignation. 'It's probably for me.'

'It's driving a silver and green Jag,' Marie told him. 'He's about six feet four and huge, and looks like something rich and rare and dangerous from the days when men were men and the battle went to the strong.'

Tegan felt the colour draining away from her skin.

'Who is it?' her mother asked urgently. 'Shall we send him away?'

Tegan gave a ghost of a smile. 'I doubt if you could. He's the determined sort.'

'Do you want to see him?' There was a steely note in her father's voice.

After a moment's indecision Tegan said with a twisted smile, 'Yes, of course I do.'

Directing a hard look at her daughter, Marie nodded, apparently satisfied, before going out of the room. Tegan sat without moving, her whole attention focused on the sound of Kieran's deep tones.

After a moment her mother's voice became louder. She was bringing him to the dining-room. Tegan's hand clenched, was covered for a second by her father's firm grip, and then Marie was saying as she came into the room, 'Of course you must eat with us! As you can see, we haven't started yet, and even if we had it wouldn't make any difference. The fish was caught about an hour ago, and there is plenty for one more. Tegan, why don't you set another place for Kieran?'

Tegan blessed her mother. Setting his place gave her something to do while Marie introduced Kieran to her husband. Of course Tegan should have done that, but her brain had collapsed into crumbs and she was sure that if she spoke all that would emerge would be a croak.

Then Kieran said, 'Hello, Tegan.'

Cornered, she flicked a quick glance upwards. The sea-coloured eyes were amused, almost mocking, but there was a white line around his mouth that didn't augur well. 'Kieran,' she said huskily.

Her mother urged hospitably, 'Do sit down and admire Rhys's fish—according to him it was dragged on board only after a mammoth battle.'

Not for the first time Tegan admired her mother's ability to make the best of a sticky situation. She herself was no use at all, but within five minutes the other three were eating and talking as though this were a normal dinner party with people who liked each other.

Slowly Tegan relaxed enough to hold her end up. However, Kieran's behaviour disturbed her. He seemed to be setting out to charm her parents while making it clear, though never too obvious, that he and Tegan knew each other well, and had been going out together for the past several months.

Bewildered and extremely suspicious, she did what she could about damage control, but when he told them of the trip to Australia to hear the Italian tenor sing his ravishing arias she sent him a dagger-sharp glance, wordlessly demanding that he shut up.

A sardonic smile didn't soften his hard mouth. Ignoring her silent command, he continued skilfully weaving his web. No one listening to him could doubt that he and Tegan were 'very good friends'. Bitterly aware of her parents' unconcealed interest, she simmered with anger.

And at the bottom, imperfectly concealed by hurt and resentment, there was joy, pure and simple, the delight of his presence. Oh, you've got it bad, she scolded her unrepentant heart. Kieran looked tired, the faint lines in his forehead a little deeper than they had been, but even so that tigerish, prowling vitality was barely leashed.

Why was he here?

He certainly wasn't giving any reasons. After dinner he seemed perfectly content to talk to them in the sitting-room, even going so far as to ask, 'Did Tegan decorate this?'

'Yes.' Marie looked proudly at her daughter. 'About five years ago. We love it.'

Very smoothly he responded, 'She has great talent. My house is all that I wanted of it.'

Irritated with being spoken of as though she weren't there, Tegan said crisply, 'I had excellent materials to work with. Raintree House is magnificent.'

Kieran's smile was distinctly subversive. 'Don't sell yourself short.' He looked at Marie. 'I wonder whether I could borrow your daughter for an hour or so? There are things we have to discuss.'

Marie's eyebrows shot up. She looked consideringly from his dark, touch face to her daughter's shuttered one. 'Why don't you ask her yourself?'

His white teeth showed for a second in what could have passed for a smile. 'Because she'd probably say no.'

'I'm not so—stupidly uncooperative,' Tegan said shortly, getting to her feet. She angled her chin at him. 'Where do you want to go? I warn you, there's precious little night life around here.'

'Come for a walk on the beach with me.'

'All right. I'll just get a jacket.'

She came back into the room to the sound of laughter, and suffered a strange pang of alienation, a pang she hastily stifled. 'I'm ready,' she announced.

As they walked across the road in the light of the streetlamp, his shrewd eyes travelled from her face to the slender lines of her body and limbs, lingering, assessing her with the cool objectivity of a man buying a horse.

'You've lost weight,' he said abruptly. 'You look far too fragile. And you're pale as a lily.'

'I'm all right.' Her voice was crisp and steady.

But in spite of that he helped her down the bank above the beach. His hand was big and warm; deliberately pulling herself free, Tegan widened the distance between them.

His mouth compressed into a taut line and for the first couple of hundred metres he didn't speak. Tegan couldn't think of a single thing to say that would break the tense silence. A few stray shorebirds darted along the beach, barely illuminated by a sliver of moon. The sea breeze was brisk. Tegan huddled inside her clothes, wondering whether his denim jacket kept the chill out.

At last she asked, 'What are you doing here?'

'Tell me about you and Sam Hoskings.'

Shock kept her silent for long moments. Then she replied wearily, 'Why? You've already made up your mind. You didn't give me a chance to explain ten years ago; why ask me now?'

'I want to hear your version.'

Baldly, with no preamble, she said, 'I didn't jilt him.'

Even in the darkness she could see the way his mouth curled. In a hard voice he said, 'Come on, Tegan, he was a friend of mine. I know what he was like after you ran out on him.'

She said quietly, hopelessly, 'I did not run out on him. I only ever thought of him as a friend.'

'He thought you loved him.'

'I liked him,' she said. 'I found him fascinating—he's a witty, brilliant man, and I admired him enormously for his courage. I suppose I was flattered that he found me interesting; at that time he was in all the newspapers. But I didn't love him; I never said I did.' She flushed, but continued bleakly, 'At first I didn't even realise—until he got so jealous. He hated me not being with him, he couldn't bear to think of me talking to anyone else—he used to go into a rage if I just rang my parents. He frightened me, so I said I'd have to stop seeing him. That was when he told me he had a right to behave like that because he loved me! I was shocked. After all, he was confined to a wheelchair; how could he fall in love? It sounds horrible but I was young, and self-centred, and incredibly naïve.'

'So what happened then?' His voice was level, as expressionless as his face, a mask sculpted in angular, unforgiving bronze.

Tegan felt the first slow, cold shivers of despair, but she had to keep trying. 'It was dreadful. He used what I can see now was emotional blackmail—I had made him love me, he needed me to survive, all that sort of thing. Somehow he managed to convince me that I owed it to him to marry him, that it was all my fault. I let him persuade me into getting engaged. He promised it would be a private engagement, but the next thing he'd bought me a ring and told the newspapers, and there was a horrible fanfare going on. I was frantic.'

'Why didn't you just tell him it was over, and make it stick?'

She looked along the white curl of the beach, trying to convey in a muted voice just how it had been for her then. 'I came to my senses almost immediately, but whenever I tried to tell him he insisted I was just young and nervous. I wasn't to worry, he kept saying, it would be all right, he would take care of everything. I couldn't get through to him. He kept telling me I made him so happy, he needed me so much, I was never to leave him because he couldn't live without me. He wanted me to move in with him, so that he could keep an eye on me, make sure no one bothered me. I realised that it would mean I'd have no privacy, no freedom, I'd be a prisoner. I felt the walls closing around me.' She stopped, unable to carry on. Keeping her face averted, she cleared her throat, forcing herself to calm down before she resumed.

'As soon as Mum read Sam's announcement in the papers she came up to Auckland. I told her what was happening, and she said he had no right to put such pressure on me. She came with me when I went to tell Sam that it was over. He had to believe her, although he didn't want to; he kept saying she'd influenced me, then when he realised I really meant it he called me—well, it doesn't matter now.' She swallowed the lump in her throat.

'And then I came.' He sounded remote, as remote as the moon and the stars and the wild white wings of a seabird flying overhead, its cry ringing over the hard-packed sand.

Tegan nodded, already tasting the acid of defeat. 'Yes, then you came. And you believed everything Sam told you.'

'He was my friend. I felt sorry for him, and furious with the little bitch who had brought him to that pass. Why didn't you try to defend yourself?' His tone was completely non-committal.

Wondering whether she had made any impact on his disbelief, she looked up at his coolly guarded face with its classic features emphasised by that unsettling authority. As always, it was impossible to read his thoughts.

With a stifled sigh she looked away. 'If you remember, I didn't get much chance. Why drag it all up now?'

'To see whether your version of what happened agreed with Sam's,' he said.

Outraged, she asked grittily, 'And does it?'

'No.' He was silent for a moment. 'No, he still sticks to the fact that you promised to marry him, and then jilted him when you realised just what marriage to a cripple would mean. No consummated sex, in other words.'

She spun around and set off back to the house. Kieran caught her up within a few strides, stopping her by wrapping long fingers around her upper arm.

'Where do you think you're going?' he demanded curtly, swivelling her to face him.

'Back home. I am not going to stay here and be insulted.' Her tone deliberately haughty, she stared into his dark face with open, flaring antagonism.

He laughed. 'Why don't you ask whether I believe him?' he said between his teeth. 'No, that would make it too easy. You want to believe the worst of me—you have right from the start. That's why you fell for Andrea's totally screwball ideas. Yesterday, when I was threatening your whereabouts out of your friend Blair, I asked her what the hell was going on in your head but all she would say was that I'd have to find out for myself. What *is* it with you?'

Tegan hesitated, but she had to tell him. Seeing him again, held like this, so close that she could sense him on her skin, had reactivated all the old longings. Whatever happened, whatever he thought of her, she loved him. Nothing could alter that fundamental fact. She would try once more to make him understand.

Searching for the right words, discarding more than she found, she said remotely, 'It seems stupid, but I've always been afraid of being taken over. My mother was well on her way to being an actress when she met my father. She'd won a scholarship to a famous British academy of drama. She tossed it in and came here to live with him.' She looked away, her profile edged in silver by the moon. 'I've always wondered whether she regretted it. We talked about it this weekend, oddly enough.'

'And?'

She told him what Marie had said, ending, 'I wasn't very old when I decided then that love was a prison, one I'd never have anything to do with again. The episode with Sam reinforced that decision.'

'And my clumsy, heavy-handed behaviour turned you off totally. Do you know why I was so angry with you that day?'

Chilled, she replied, 'Because I'd hurt Sam so badly.'

'Partly. But mostly because I took one look at you and to my utter and complete horror and astonishment realised that I wanted to take you away somewhere and make love to you until you'd never see another man without my face being superimposed on his, never make love with another man without remembering how you felt, how I felt when I took you.'

Her head jerked up. Searching his face with eyes attuned to the night, Tegan read confirmation of what he had just said. 'Then why—why were you so cruel?' she asked in a shattered little voice.

'Because Sam was a friend, and he was in love with you, and you didn't even realise what you'd done to him. You were an innocent young Circe, unaware of your power, thoughtlessly cruel, yet in spite of everything, in spite of the fact that Sam and I had been friends since childhood, I couldn't take my eyes off you. And you looked at me with fear and hatred.' Although his smile was cruel and mocking the mockery was self-directed. 'It had never happened to me before, that instant, fatal attraction, and I didn't want it to happen then. I wasn't exactly rational, or thinking logically.'

Tegan looked up sharply. 'So when we met again you decided you'd rid yourself of this itch.'

'Yes,' he said on a wry note. His voice dropped, smooth as run honey yet sending shivers up her spine. 'Your elusiveness roused my hunting instincts.'

Flames kindled in the golden depths of her eyes. 'Did you know I was a partner in Decorators Inc when you made me plead to do the job?'

'Yes. I was testing you, seeing how far you would go. It gave me a bitter kind of satisfaction to find that although you so patently didn't want anything to do with me you were prepared to beg for the job.'

'Only because I owed it to Blair,' she retorted.

'How?'

She said uneasily, 'It's difficult to explain.'

'Try me.'

She sent a fleeting glance upwards. The cutting lines of his profile testified to strength and determination. She said, 'I wanted to keep things going. It was all I could do for her. It sounds stupid——'

'No, it makes sense.' He released her and when she automatically began to walk back along the beach he fell into step beside her.

In silence they walked towards a craggy headland, the sand squeaking slightly beneath them. The air was cool and salt-scented, crisp with the promise of autumn. On the horizon the Mercury Islands were black silhouettes against a silver sea. Tegan didn't know how to feel. He had not said that he loved her. What if he had come down to ask her to resume their affair, if making love once could be called an affair?

When Kieran spoke again his voice was filled with raw emotion. 'I was torn in two. Within a very short time I knew damned well that the pagan enchantment hadn't faded—it was as strong as ever. I was being disloyal to Sam, but after a few days I didn't give a damn. But I didn't want to hear you talk about him, I didn't want to listen to you lie. I kept you from telling me anything about it because that way I could delude myself into thinking that you were what you seemed to be—honest and passionate and very, very aware of me.'

'If—if you wanted me so much, why did you start to make love to me that last time then stop, and leave? That was cruel.'

The passionate fury vibrating though her question startled her, but he met her anger and frustration with an equal intensity.

'As cruel as believing my sister's half-cocked theories? By then I'd hoped we'd laid the ghosts of the past, but when you listened to her you showed you didn't trust me at all; it was just physical. I felt completely betrayed. So I took you without any tenderness—at least, I tried to. Only you surrendered so sweetly, so generously, that my anger was transmuted into desire. And I knew I couldn't do that to you—take you contemptuously and walk away. I had to go.'

Wincing, Tegan retorted defensively, 'I didn't want to believe Andrea! But it seemed so logical—she had it all worked out. You didn't show any interest in me until after Rick had talked to me, and each deepening of our relationship seemed to come after some incident with him.'

'Did it?' he asked roughly. 'I don't remember. Perhaps it was because his open appreciation warned me that there were plenty of men out there who wanted you. That cub you were going out with when we met again, for one.'

The breeze from the sea was brisk and cooling, blowing tendrils of hair about her face. Slowly she said, 'There haven't been many men.'

'Why not tell me the truth? There weren't any men before me, were there?'

Lying was useless. 'No,' she admitted, relieved that the friendly darkness hid her hot cheeks. 'How did you know?'

'It was fairly obvious that the whole experience was entirely new to you. Why, Tegan?'

She ran the tip of her tongue along her bottom lip. It tasted faintly of salt. 'You weren't the only one who looked and liked what they saw, that first time we met,' she at last admitted with a glimmering, reluctant smile. 'After that I judged every man against you, and no one measured up.'

He laughed softly, without humour. 'What fools we've been, you and I.' His hands around her face were warm and firm, tilting it so that he could see the emotions she was trying so hard to keep under control.

'I should have known,' he said, almost on a note of wonder, 'when one smile from you began to mean much more to me than my work, or anything else in my smug, self-satisfied life. Instead, I told myself that it was lust, and that I could take you and leave you when it was sated, and go back to being the man I'd been before. Then we made love, and I realised it wasn't mere lust, or desire; it had become transmuted into something else, something I'd never experienced before. But although you made love with all the abandon of a Circe there were still barriers.'

'I was afraid,' she confessed, hardly daring to hope, yet aware that he was admitting to much more than the lust he had spoken of.

'So was I. I'd been engaged, and broken it off when I realised that all we felt for each other was a strong physical attraction. Kirsty was intelligent and entertaining and beautiful, she would have made a perfectly suitable wife, but I felt nothing beyond a superficial affection, and she wasn't interested in anything beyond her work and the sex. It's selfish, but I wanted a woman who'd love me more than anything else, who would put me first. I'd begun to lose hope of ever finding someone like that, and then I met you again. Everything screeched to a sudden halt; I went through the lot, bells ringing and celestial choirs singing, my heart leaping about in my chest like a fresh-caught salmon—and it was so obvious you didn't feel the same way.'

His thumb moved slowly over her lips, a faint roughness making them tingle. 'You must have known I wanted you,' she said, a catch in her voice.

'Oh, yes, but what I felt for you was infinitely greater than wanting,' he said sombrely. 'I knew I'd have to take things slowly; you were still very suspicious, and with reason. But by the time I left for El Amir I thought we had grown to know each other, to understand each other. I was going to ask you to marry me. When we made love,' he said deeply, 'it shook my world off its foundations. Until then I had no idea what a man and a woman could do for each other.'

Colour heated her skin, and she sent him a smoky golden glance, enjoying the quick flames that leapt to new heights in his gaze.

His chest lifted with a sudden inflow of breath. He lifted her hands to his mouth and kissed them, his mouth lingering on the soft hollow of her palm, biting gently at the mount of Venus below her thumb. Strange, erotic little chills ran through her.

'You gave yourself so freely to me, with such innocent, glorious abandon, that I began to allow myself the luxury of thinking that perhaps this was love, that I'd found the one woman I could trust, who'd trust me. I should have asked you to marry me then.'

'Why didn't you?'

He shrugged. 'My bloody suspicious nature again, I suppose. I wish to heaven I had; it would have saved both of us a lot of pain. I was testing you again. I wanted all of your loyalty. I was even jealous of Blair.

'It's no excuse, but in our childhood there were so many secrets, so little loyalty. You were loyal to Blair, but you had none for me.'

'I wondered why anyone as wonderful as you could fall in love with me.'

His hands tightened. Beneath his lashes his eyes were slivers of fire, blue-green, hot as the heart of the sun. 'I didn't realise that you had your insecurities, my pagan enchantress. You always seemed so confident.'

Her smile was wobbly. She had to tell him now that she was not going to give up her job because he wanted her whole attention. She loved him with all of her heart, but she could not be caged by her love into a lesser life.

Aloud she said, 'I do have other loyalties, Kieran. I can't just cut them off——'

'I'm not that stupid,' he said, such stark sincerity in his tone that she believed him, and a fear so deeply embedded within her that until then she hadn't even realised its existence withered and died. 'And although I'm possessive I'm not twisted. I don't want to monitor your every thought, make your life hideous with jealousy, or ever stop you from doing what you want to. I just want to love you, to cherish you, to walk with you through the rest of my life, wake in the night to hear you breathing beside me and feel your warmth on my skin. That's all. Now, my heart, my dearest witch, do you think you can put me out of my misery and tell me that you love me, that you'll marry me as soon as possible, and that we are going to live happily ever after?'

'I can't promise the happy ever after,' she whispered, joy filling her so much that she thought she might choke on it. 'That's out of my hands, but I can promise to love you until the day I die.'

'I like the sound of that,' he said, smiling. His hand stroked tenderly down the length of her throat, setting off delicious little shudders. His face hardened with the intensity of desire. 'I love you, you beautiful torment. I never thought I'd say that to any woman. I love you infinitely more than I ever thought I could love a woman, and I need you, and I promise to make you as happy as I can.'

'But what about Sam?' she asked, frowning.

His wide shoulders moved in a shrug. 'I like Sam, but I love you. If he can't accept the situation I'll be sorry, but you are my life, the light at the heart of my being, the only hope I have for paradise.'

Need began to pulse deeply inside her. She lifted her face in mute invitation, and gave him her mouth, and with it her heart and her future.

His dark face swam before her vision, no longer closed from her. She could read his emotions as clearly as her own. How strange, Tegan thought, before she yielded completely and stopped thinking, how wonderful that love was so easy to accept, once you surrendered to it.

POSTCARDS FROM EUROPE

HARLEQUIN PRESENTS®

Hi—

I'm in trouble—I'm engaged to Stuart, but I suddenly wish my relationship with Jan Breydel wasn't strictly business. Perhaps it's simply the fairy-tale setting of Bruges. Belgium is such a romantic country!

Love, Geraldine

Travel across Europe in 1994 with Harlequin Presents. Collect a new Postcards From Europe title each month!

Don't miss
THE BRUGES ENGAGEMENT
by Madeleine Ker
Harlequin Presents #1650

Available in May, wherever Harlequin Presents books are sold.

HPPPE5

MILLION DOLLAR SWEEPSTAKES (III)

No purchase necessary. To enter the sweepstakes and receive the Free Books and Surprise Gift, follow the directions published and complete and mail your "Win A Fortune" Game Card. If not taking advantage of the book and gift offer or if the "Win A Fortune" Game Card is missing, you may enter by hand-printing your name and address on a 3" X 5" card and mailing it (limit: one entry per envelope) via First Class Mail to: Million Dollar Sweepstakes (III) "Win A Fortune" Game, P.O. Box 1867, Buffalo, NY 14269-1867, or Million Dollar Sweepstakes (III) "Win A Fortune" Game, P.O. Box 609, Fort Erie, Ontario L2A 5X3. When your entry is received, you will be assigned sweepstakes numbers. To be eligible entries must be received no later than March 31, 1996. No liability is assumed for printing errors or lost, late or misdirected entries. Odds of winning are determined by the number of eligible entries distributed and received.

Sweepstakes open to residents of the U.S. (except Puerto Rico), Canada, Europe and Taiwan who are 18 years of age or older. All applicable laws and regulations apply. Sweepstakes offer void wherever prohibited by law. Values of all prizes are in U.S.currency. This sweepstakes is presented by Torstar Corp, its subsidiaries and affiliates, in conjunction with book, merchandise and/or product offerings. For a copy of the official rules governing this sweepstakes offer, send a self-addressed, stamped envelope (WA residents need not affix return postage) to: MILLION DOLLAR SWEEPSTAKES (III) Rules, P.O. Box 4573, Blair, NE 68009, USA.

SWP-H494

HARLEQUIN ®

PRESENTS Plus

Meet Alex Hamilton. His reputation as a lady's man convinces Marly to teach Alex a lesson he won't soon forget. But the tables turn when Marly realizes she's become the student—and that she's learning how to love!

And then there's Reid Bannerman. Annys quickly discovers that three weeks at sea with Reid, her ex-husband, is a long time to spend together—especially when the quarters are close and the attraction between them still sizzles!

Alex and Reid are just two of the sexy men you'll fall in love with each month in Harlequin Presents Plus.

Watch for
GIVE A MAN A BAD NAME by Roberta Leigh
Harlequin Presents Plus #1647
and
FLAME ON THE HORIZON by Daphne Clair
Harlequin Presents Plus #1648

Harlequin Presents Plus
The best has just gotten better!

Available in May wherever Harlequin books are sold.

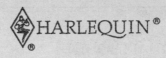

Harlequin Books requests the pleasure of your company this June in Eternity, Massachusetts, for WEDDINGS, INC.

For generations, couples have been coming to Eternity, Massachusetts, to exchange wedding vows. Legend has it that those married in Eternity's chapel are destined for a lifetime of happiness. And the residents are more than willing to give the legend a hand.

Beginning in June, you can experience the legend of Eternity. Watch for one title per month, across all of the Harlequin series.

HARLEQUIN BOOKS... NOT THE SAME OLD STORY!

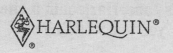

Harlequin proudly presents four stories about
convenient but not *conventional* reasons for marriage:

- ◆ To save your godchildren from a
  "wicked stepmother"

- ◆ To help out your eccentric aunt—and her sexy
  business partner

- ◆ To bring an old man happiness by making him
  a grandfather

- ◆ To escape from a ghostly existence and become a
  real woman

Marriage By Design—four brand-new stories by four
of Harlequin's most popular authors:

CATHY GILLEN THACKER
JASMINE CRESSWELL
GLENDA SANDERS
MARGARET CHITTENDEN

Don't miss this exciting collection of stories about
marriages of convenience. Available in April, wherever
Harlequin books are sold.

This June, Harlequin invites you to a wedding of

Promised Brides

Celebrate the joy and romance of weddings past with PROMISED BRIDES—a collection of original historical short stories, written by three best-selling historical authors:

The Wedding of the Century—MARY JO PUTNEY
Jesse's Wife—KRISTIN JAMES
The Handfast—JULIE TETEL

Three unforgettable heroines, three award-winning authors! PROMISED BRIDES is available in June wherever Harlequin Books are sold.

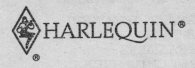

HARLEQUIN®

Relive the romance....
Harlequin is proud to bring you

A new collection of three complete novels every month. By the most requested authors, featuring the most requested themes.

Available in May:

Three handsome, successful, unmarried men are about to get the surprise of their lives.... Well, better late than never!

Three complete novels in one special collection:

DESIRE'S CHILD by Candace Schuler
INTO THE LIGHT by Judith Duncan
A SUMMER KIND OF LOVE by Shannon Waverly

Available at you're retail outlet from

HREQ5

HARLEQUIN®

Don't miss these Harlequin favorites by some of our most
distinguished authors!
And now, you can receive a discount by ordering two or more titles!

HT #25551	THE OTHER WOMAN by Candace Schuler	$2.99	☐
HT #25539	FOOLS RUSH IN by Vicki Lewis Thompson	$2.99	☐
HP #11550	THE GOLDEN GREEK by Sally Wentworth	$2.89	☐
HP #11603	PAST ALL REASON by Kay Thorpe	$2.99	☐
HR #03228	MEANT FOR EACH OTHER by Rebecca Winters	$2.89	☐
HR #03268	THE BAD PENNY by Susan Fox	$2.99	☐
HS #70532	TOUCH THE DAWN by Karen Young	$3.39	☐
HS #70540	FOR THE LOVE OF IVY by Barbara Kaye	$3.39	☐
HI #22177	MINDGAME by Laura Pender	$2.79	☐
HI #22214	TO DIE FOR by M.J. Rodgers	$2.89	☐
HAR #16421	HAPPY NEW YEAR, DARLING by Margaret St. George	$3.29	☐
HAR #16507	THE UNEXPECTED GROOM by Muriel Jensen	$3.50	☐
HH #28774	SPINDRIFT by Miranda Jarrett	$3.99	☐
HH #28782	SWEET SENSATIONS by Julie Tetel	$3.99	☐

Harlequin Promotional Titles

#83259	UNTAMED MAVERICK HEARTS	$4.99	☐
	(Short-story collection featuring Heather Graham Pozzessere, Patricia Potter, Joan Johnston)		

(limited quantities available on certain titles)

	AMOUNT	$
DEDUCT:	10% DISCOUNT FOR 2+ BOOKS	$
	POSTAGE & HANDLING	$
	($1.00 for one book, 50¢ for each additional)	
	APPLICABLE TAXES*	$ _____
	TOTAL PAYABLE	$ _____
	(check or money order—please do not send cash)	

To order, complete this form and send it, along with a check or money order for the
total above, payable to Harlequin Books, to: **In the U.S.:** 3010 Walden Avenue,
P.O. Box 9047, Buffalo, NY 14269-9047; **In Canada:** P.O. Box 613, Fort Erie, Ontario,
L2A 5X3.

Name: _____

Address: _____ City: _____

State/Prov.: _____ Zip/Postal Code: _____

*New York residents remit applicable sales taxes.
Canadian residents remit applicable GST and provincial taxes.

HBACK-AJ